SNAPDRAGON

SNAPDRAGON

Kat Leyh

First Second
NEW YORK

OUR TOWN HAS A WITCH.
CAW CAW
CAW
CAW!!
SHE FED HER EYE TO THE DEVIL. SHE EATS ROADKILL AND CASTS SPELLS WITH THE BONES...
CAW
CAW
CAW

THAT'S THE KIND OF BULL THE DUMB KIDS AT MY SCHOOL SAY.
WITCHES AIN'T REAL.
SHE'S JUST AN OLD LOONY.
BUT...
...THEY ALSO SAY SHE EATS PETS.
CLENCH
GOOD BOY

SO I HAVE TO BE SURE.

PART 1: THE WITCH

AL'S SEAFOOD Bar & Grill

GOOD BOY!!

GOOD BOY!

ARK!!

YOU'RE ALIVE! I THOUGHT—
ARK! ARK!

WH-WHAT DID SHE *DO* TO YOU?!
huff
huff
huff

DON'T YOU ***KNOW?***

I'M EATING
HIM PIECE
BY PIECE...

HCK
HcHAH!!

!!
AH!
RR!!
YOU'RE A LIAR!!!

YOU'RE A LIAR AND I'M NOT AFRAID OF YOU!!

OH?
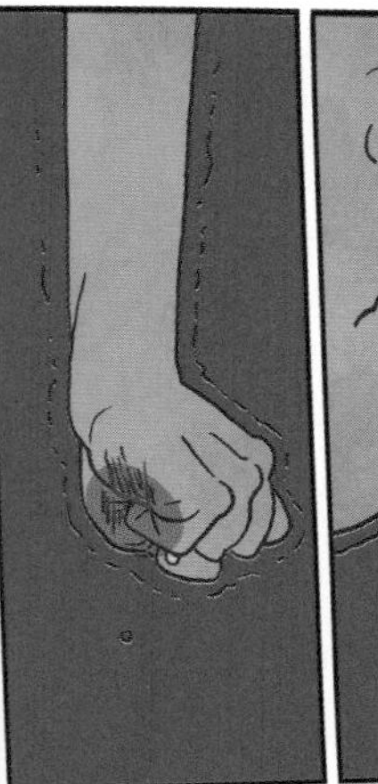

HMMM...

YOU'RE RIGHT. I DIDN'T EAT ANY PART OF YOUR DOG.

I FOUND 'IM HURT ON THE SIDE OF THE ROAD. SO I PATCHED 'IM UP.

OFF YOU GO, BRASH GIRL.
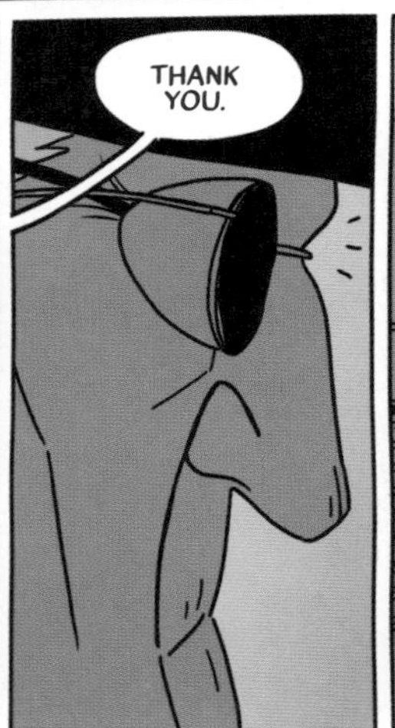
THANK YOU.

Ka-CHNK

MAMA?

BABY? WHATCHU STILL DOIN' UP?

I FOUND GOOD BOY!
OH!?

HOW WAS WORK?

...AND SHE WALKED AROUND HALF THE DAY WITH IT IN HER HAIR.
...SHE NEVER NOTICED?
NOT 'TIL WE TRIED TO ADD A SECOND!
GOT YELLED AT FOR WASTING COCKTAIL UMBRELLAS!
HAHA HAHA!

EEEEEEEE!!

OOOH, GROSS!
THERE'S GUTS!
KIRSTY! COME AND TOUCH IT!
EEW! NO!

C'MON! TOUCH IT!

HEY!

HEY! IT'S SNOTTY!
LEAVE IT ALONE!

WHY? DIDN'T EAT ENOUGH FOR LUNCH?
CAREFUL, DUDE, SHE BITES.

OH, GROSS, LOOK!

IT'S FULL OF *MAGGOTS!*

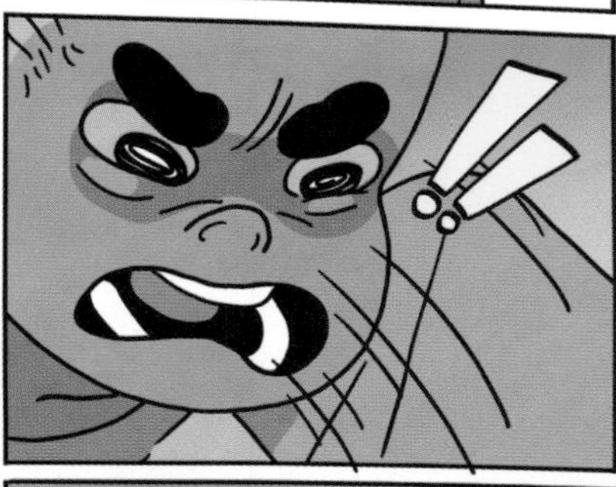

OH MY GOD!!
SICK! SHE'S DOING IT! SHE'S EATING IT!

haha HA HA haha haha ha HAHAHA

LOUIS! C'MON!

HEY. YOU OKA—

HWSSSSS!!

HEY!

SCHOOL'S NOT OUT YET!

RING-RING!

I DON'T GET MANY REPEAT VISITORS.

I KNOW YOU'RE NOT A WITCH.
OH?

YEAH. AIN'T NO SUCH THING. BUT...

WHAT AM I SUPPOSED TO DO WITH THESE?
I— YOU—
THEIR MAMA'S DEAD AND YOU HELPED ***GOOD BOY***— I THOUGHT MAYBE...

I THOUGHT MAYBE YOU COULD HELP THEM.

WELL C'MON, BRING 'EM ON INSIDE.

THEY LOOK A FEW WEEKS OLD...
THAT'S LUCKY.

...THEY'LL BE READY TO BE ON THEIR OWN IN A MONTH OR SO.
...KEEP 'EM WARM. FEED 'EM...
...THEY'LL LIKELY SURVIVE.

YOU'LL NEED TO FEED 'EM A FEW TIMES A DAY...

WH-I THOUGHT **YOU** WOULD TAKE CARE OF—

—UH.

Meowdy!
UH.
Meowdy!
POP
UUUUHHHH...
WHAT'RE YOU STARING AT, GIRL?!
NOTHING.
AND MY NAME'S SNAP.
AND WHAT KINDA NAME IS THAT?

MY NAME IS SNAPDRAGON!
THEY'RE MY MAMA'S FAVORITE FLOWER!
FAVORITE FLOWER, HM? I LIKE THAT.
ALL RIGHT, SNAPDRAGON.
MY NAME'S JACKS.
AND I GOT A DEAL FOR YOU!

I'LL KEEP THEM POSSUMS HERE. BUT YOU GOTTA TAKE CARE OF 'EM.
I'LL EVEN SHOW YOU HOW...
Meowdy!

TCH.
"...BE BACK HERE AT SIX A.M."
BLECH.
AW.
COOL.

MAMA!?
ARK!! ARK!!

HEY, G.B.

ARK!! ARK!!

crunch crunch
huff huff

Snap —
Covering a late
shift tonight!
-WALK G.B.
BEFORE DARK
- Do your homework
- Go to bed on time!!
love, MOM
RUH RUH RUH RUH RUH RUH RUH RUH

I HEAR YOU, GEEBIES!

WHY DO YOU STILL NEED TO WALK ALL THE TIME?
YOU ONLY GOT THREE LEGS!

I LIKE YOUR DOG.

OH.
IT'S
YOU.

WHAT'RE
YOU DOIN'
UP THERE?
HANG
ON!

MY BROTHERS
KICK ME OUT
OF OUR ROOM
A LOT.
I LIKE TO
HANG OUT
UP HERE.

CAN I PET 'IM?
SURE. HE'S FRIENDLY.
sniff sniff sniff

I DIDN'T WANT TO MESS WITH THAT POSSUM EARLIER...
...I WAS HAVING LUNCH WITH THOSE OTHER KIDS 'CAUSE WE PLAY BASEBA-
A'RIGHT, A'RIGHT, FINE! WHATEVER...

SO...WHAT HAPPENED TO YOUR DOG?
WHAT DO YOU MEAN?
HIS, UH, HIS LEG?
OH, THAT.

THE WITCH ATE IT.
WHAT? NUH-UH!
YEAH-HUH!

I WENT TO HER HOUSE TO SAVE HIM!
YOU DID NOT!
I DID, TOO!
Huff Huff Huff

DIDN'T!
DID!
SEE THESE SCABS? HER THORNS ATTACKED ME!
Huff Huff Huff

YEAH? THEN HOW'D YOU ESCAPE?
EASY! I WALKED BACKWARD OFF HER PROPERTY WITH MY EYES SHUT!
THAT'S THE ONLY WAY TO ESCAPE A WITCH!
OH, REALLY? AND DID YOU DO IT WITH A ROSEMARY SPRIG IN YOUR POCKET?
EVERYONE KNOWS THAT'S THE SECRET!
WAIT A SECOND....
NO! BECAUSE ROSEMARY ONLY WORKS DURING DREAM SEQUENCES!
I KNEW THAT! THAT WAS A TEST!
WHAT YOU REALLY NEED TO CARRY WITH YOU IS ANGELICA ROOT–

—BOUND WITH THE WITCH'S HAIR!

HEY, LOUIS! WHO'S YOUR LITTLE *GIRLFRIEND?*
Oof!

YOU LIKE *WEIRD ONES,* HUH, BRO?
SHUT IT, GEORGE!
GET OFF, JAIME!
SHOVE
SPACE ASSAULT

IGNORE THEM, SNAP, THEY'RE IDIOTS.
HAHAHA
haha

I DON'T THINK YOU'RE—

—HEY!
SEE YOU 'ROUND, LOUIS!

SLAM

LICK LICK

ARG!

MEOW! MEOW! MEOW!
GOOD MORNING!

MEOW!
GOOD MORNING!
MEOW!
MEOW!
MEOW!

GOOD MOR-
SMACK!

November
CREEK
MOBILE HOME PARK

Snapdragon,
Out back.
-J

OVER HERE!

YOU'RE ON TIME.

YOU SAID SIX A.M.

HMPH.

ARE THE POSSUMS OKAY?

YES.

I'LL SHOW YA HOW TO FEED THEM AFTER THE COLLECTION.

BRING THE WHEELBARROW, PLEASE.

THE *COLLECTION?!*

SO...
YOU GONNA TELL ME ***WHAT*** WE'RE COLLECTING?

AH!

TIME TO GO.

UUUH... ARE YOU TALKING TO **ME?**

HUSH.

WAKE UP!!
SCRAAAPE!!
NOW WE GO.

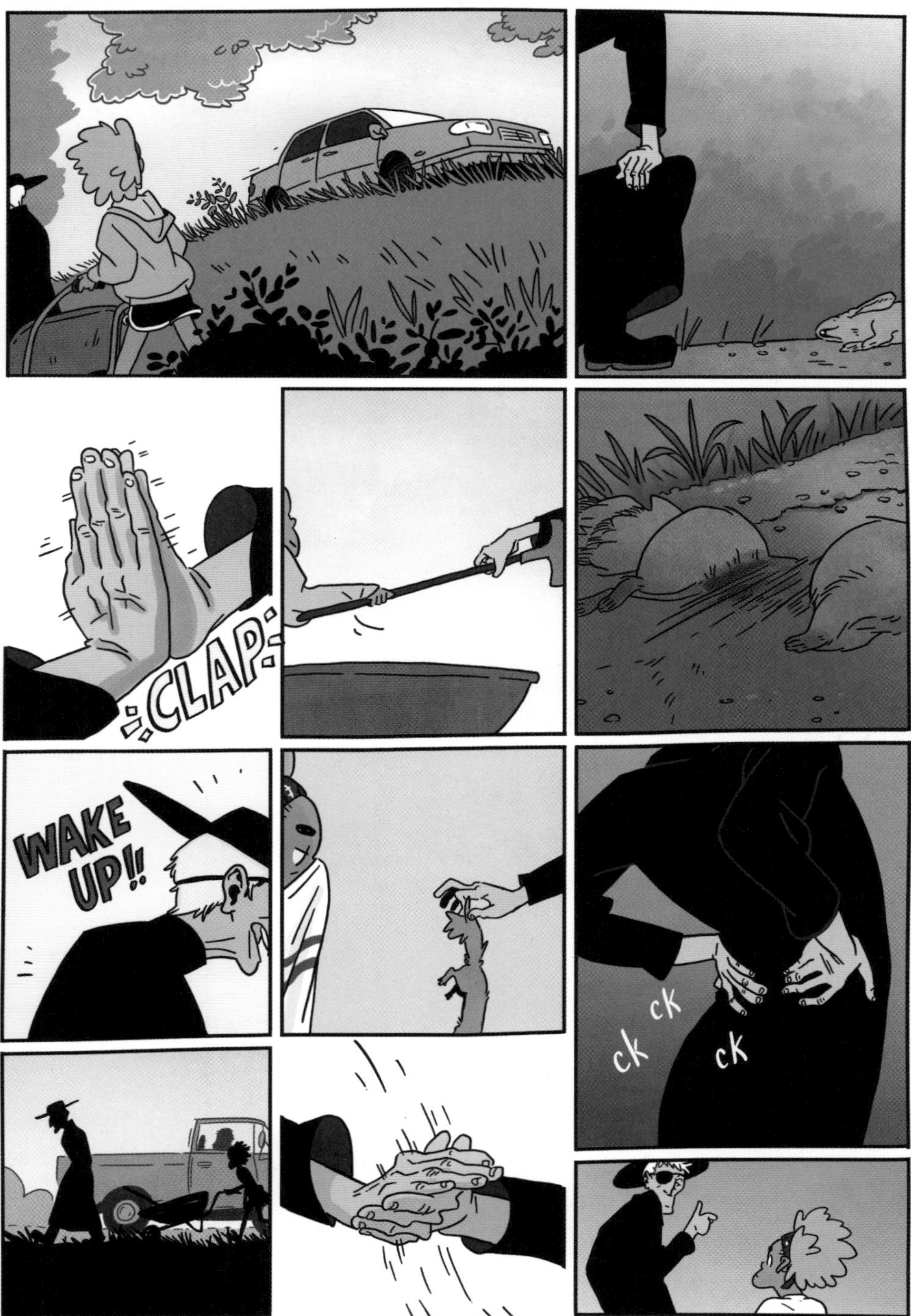
CLAP
WAKE UP!!
ck ck ck

...

I CAN'T TAKE IT!!

WHEN ARE YOU GONNA TELL ME WHAT YOU *DO* WITH THESE?!
DO YOU *EAT* 'EM?!
USE 'EM FOR *SPELLS?!*
WHAT?!

"SPELLS"?

I THOUGHT *I* WASN'T A WITCH?

HCK HCK HCK
YOU'RE A STORMY ONE.
I'D WONDERED WHEN YOU'D ASK.
WELL? COME ON.

SUPPOSE IT WAS TOO FOGGY THIS MORNING TO SEE.

I LET 'EM SIT OUT HERE 'TIL THEY'RE JUST BONES, AND THEN—

WELL, I'LL SHOW YOU THE NEXT PART IN THE HOUSE.

ALSO, THERE'S TEA!

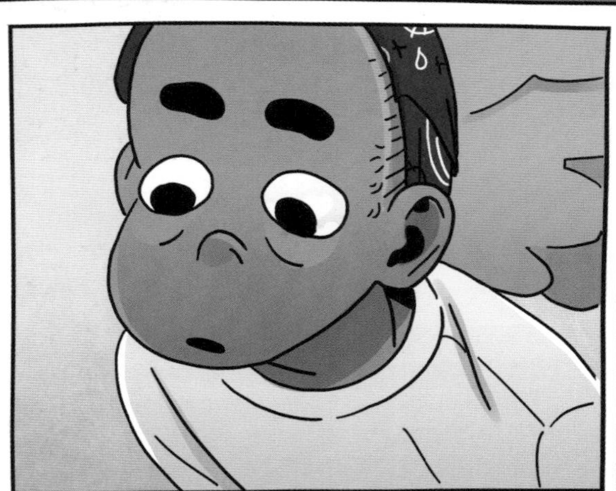

sluu uuurrrrrpp

THAT FELLA'S A COYOTE.

SO THIS IS WHAT YOU DO WITH THE ROADKILL?
BURY 'EM 'TIL THEY'RE BONES, THEN... PUT 'EM BACK TOGETHER?
YEP, THAT'S ABOUT IT.
"ARTICULATION" IS WHAT IT'S CALLED.

LEFT RIGHT

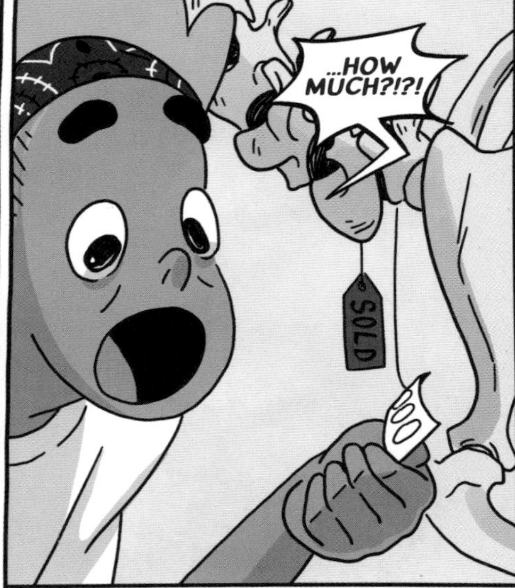

WHO SPENDS THAT MUCH ON OLD BONES?!
M.R.DUCKS

LOTTA COLLECTORS, EDUCATORS... A FEW MUSEUMS.
I SELL 'EM ON THE INTERNETS.
BUY BONES HERE
M.R.DUCKS

WOW.

I NEVER MET AN OLD PERSON WHO COULD USE THE *INTERNET.*

SO THAT'S WHAT ALL THIS IS...
I *KNEW* YOU WEREN'T A WITCH! *HA!*
...IT'S JUST A BUSINESS!
A REALLY WEIRD BUSINESS!

A REALLY, REALLY, REALLY, REALLY, *REALLY*—

—REALLY—
OKAY.

BUT THEN... WHAT WAS ALL THAT CLAPPING ABOUT?

THAT'S ENOUGH FOR NOW.
oh, c'mon!
M.R.D.

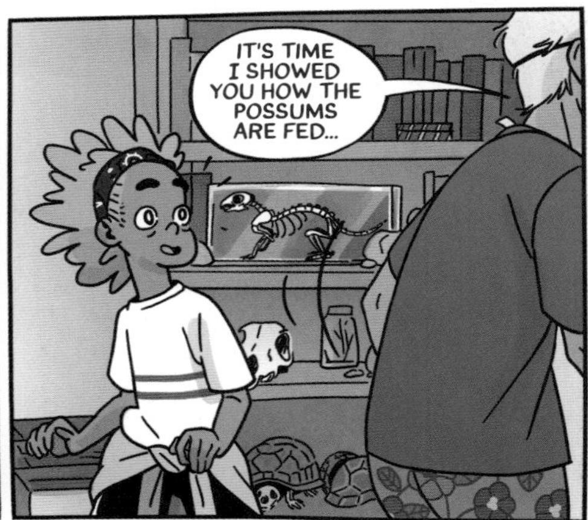
IT'S TIME I SHOWED YOU HOW THE POSSUMS ARE FED...

UNLESS MY WORK'S TOO CREEPY FOR YOU AND YOU WANT TO QUIT?
HELL NO, MA'AM!
"VOLUNTEER WORK?"

ROOK'S BOOKS
YEAH. HELPIN' AN OLD LADY WITH CHORES AND STUFF.
1115
ROOK'S BOOKS

THAT'S REAL NICE, BABY!
MM-HM.
ARE YOU DONE YET, MAMA?

NOT YET.
BUT I'M *HUNGRYYY!*
WE'LL GET FOOD WHEN I'M DONE.
GO LOOK AROUND.
SALE

UUUURRGH.
SALE

YOU FIND EVERYTHING OKAY?
YEAH, THANKS. I'LL TAKE THESE.
WITH THE STUDENT DISCOUNT.

AND THIS ONE!

SALE
COMPARATIVE ANATOMY of VERTEBRATES
OH, HONEY...
THIS ISN'T A NICE BOOK FOR LITTLE GIRLS.
WE HAVE A LOT OF CUTE BOOKS ABOUT ANIMALS!

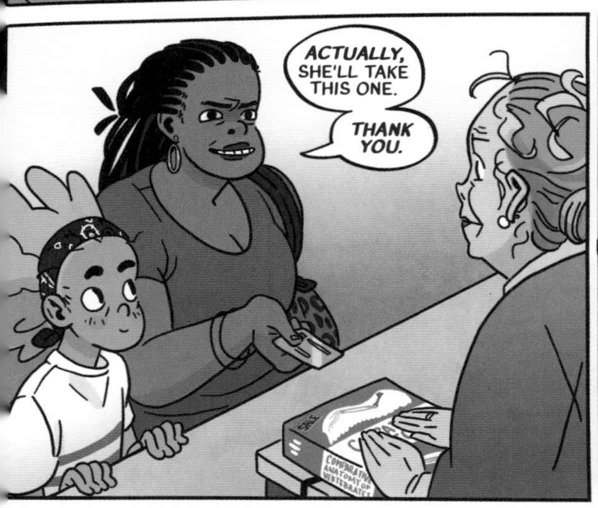
ACTUALLY, SHE'LL TAKE THIS ONE.
THANK YOU.
SALE
COMPARATIVE ANATOMY OF VERTEBRATES

WHICH DO YOU THINK HAS MORE BONES: A HUMAN OR A MOUSE?

HMM... HUMAN?
RUH RUH RUH RUH RUH RUH... RUH RUH

MICE! THEY GOT A BUNCH MORE VERTEBRAE THAN WE DO 'CAUSE OF THEIR TAILS!
AH.
DID YOU KNOW WHALES HAVE THE SAME ARM BONES PEOPLE HAVE? IN THEIR FLIPPERS?
REALLY?

YEAH, AND SO DO BATS! THEIR WINGS ARE LIKE GIANT HANDS WITH REEALLY LONG FINGERS!
THAT'S CREEPY.
I THINK IT'S COOL!

A'RIGHT, A'RIGHT, DOCTOR BLOOM—
BOOK DOWN. TIME FOR DINNER.

WHICH PIECE YOU WANT?
CHICK CHICK

FEMUR, PLEASE!

THAT'S THE—
LEG BONE. YEAH, YOUR MAMA KNOWS SOME STUFF, TOO.

GOOD BOY
SO WHAT'S ALL THIS FOR? SCHOOL PROJECT?
I JUST THINK IT'S INTERESTING.

chew
chew
chew

YOU BEEN MAKIN' ANY NEW FRIENDS AT SCHOOL?
NAH.
I'M OKAY ON MY OWN.
OH?

EVERYONE THINKS I'M WEIRD.
YOU SURE THAT'S WHAT ***EVERYONE*** THINKS...

—OR IS THAT WHAT YOU'RE ***AFRAID*** OF?

I DON'T LIKE YOU HERE ON YOUR OWN ALL THE TIME.

I WANT YOU TO INVITE A FRIEND OVER.

BUT ***MAMAAA!***

SNAPDRAGON.

I'M NOT RAISIN' AN ANTISOCIAL.

CHICK CHICK

I BETCHU CAN THINK OF ***SOMEONE.***

CHRIS?

CHRIS!!
Chris
BABE. WHAT'RE YOU DOING HERE?

KIMBERLY! WHAT ARE YOU DOING HERE?

PLEASE DON'T GO IN THERE!

HAHA. YOU'RE NOT SCARED OF **THE WITCH,** ARE YOU?

I HAVE A BAD FEELING ABOUT THIS PLACE!

RELAX, BABE. I'LL BE FINE.

WRONG!

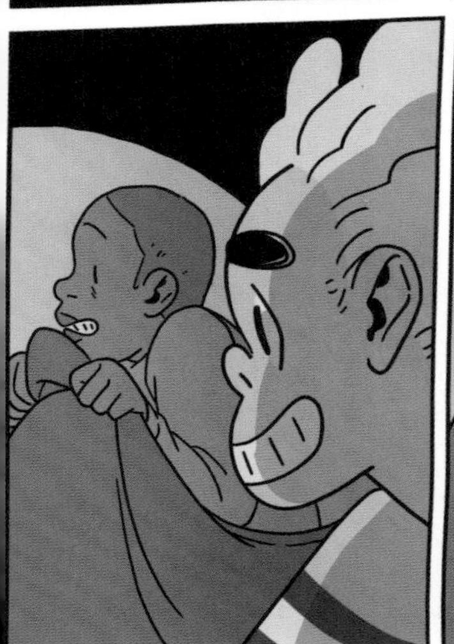

THANKS FOR INVITING ME OVER TO WATCH THIS MOVIE, SNAP.
SURE. WATCHING YOU GET SCARED HAS ACTUALLY BEEN PRETTY *FUN!*
MY MOM ***NEVER*** LETS ME WATCH THESE AT HOME. SHE THINKS *I'LL* GET NIGHTMARES.
MY MOM WON'T BE HOME FOR AN HOUR STILL!

DO YOU GET LONELY?
BEIN' HOME ALONE ALL THE TIME?
sniff
sniff sniff

ARK! ARK!
NOT SINCE I GOT ***GOOD BOY!***
HE USED TO BELONG TO MY MAMA'S OLD BOYFRIEND—

—CHUCK.
huff
huff
huff

HE SUCKED?
SO HARD!

BUT MY MAMA BOOTED HIM, AND I GOT G.B.!

SO NOW IT'S THE THREE OF US AND THAT'S JUST FINE BY M—

—OH YES, THIS IS THE BEST PART!!!
AAAAAAAAAAAAH!!!

AAHH!!!
HAHA

HA
HA

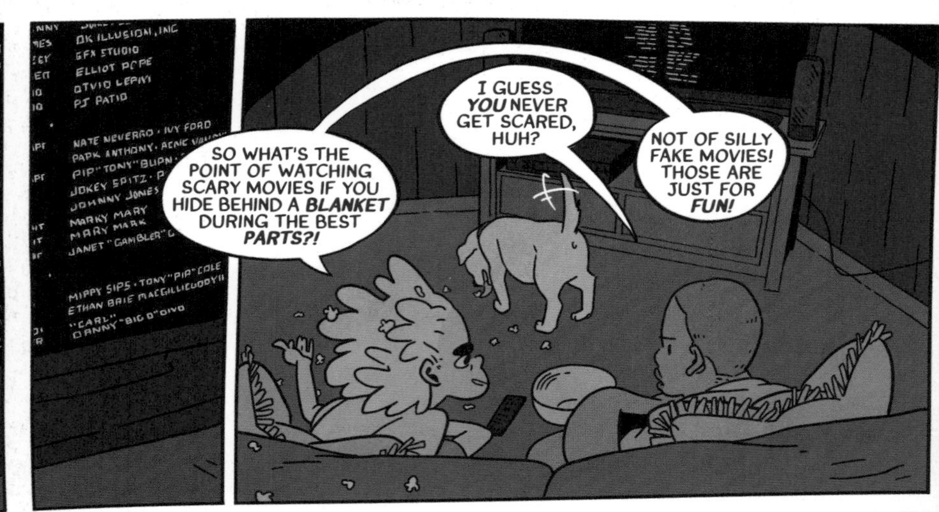

NOW, ***REAL*** MONSTERS...

PFT. WHAT D'YOU ***MEAN*** "REAL"?

WELL...

FOR ***GENERATIONS,*** MY FAMILY HAS BEEN ***STALKED...***

...BY A ***MONSTER...***

WHAT?!

TELL ME!

WE ***CALL*** IT...

ONE-EYED TOM

"MY GRANNY WAS THE FIRST TO SEE IT."

"IT WAS SO FOGGY THAT NIGHT, SHE ENDED UP ON A ROAD SHE DIDN'T RECOGNIZE."

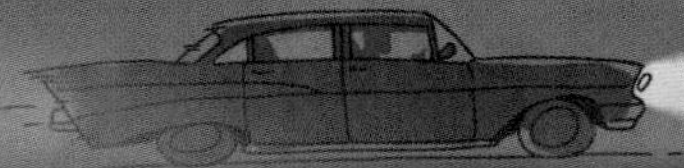

"AND TO MAKE IT WORSE–"

"–THE DEFROSTER HAD STOPPED WORKING."
ARG!

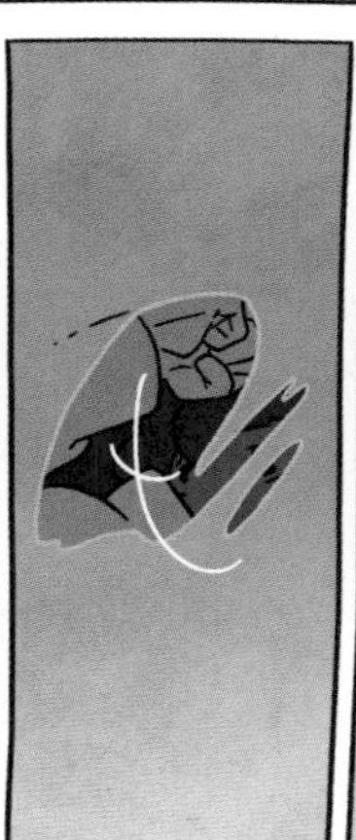

SCREEEEEEEE

"SHE'D SEEN..."

"...*SOMETHING*..."

"...BUT WASN'T SURE WHAT."

"SHE GOT OUT TO MAKE SURE IT WASN'T ANOTHER PERSON."
HELLO?

"BUT THEN HER FLASHLIGHT DIED!"
thnk
thnk
thnk
"PSH. NO WAY!"
"SHUT UP, LOU!"

"AND THEN SHE SAW IT."

"JUST BEYOND THE REACH OF HER HEADLIGHTS, THE SHAPE OF SOMETHING..."

"...MOVING TOWARD HER."

"IT HAD ONE EYE..."
"...AND IT WASN'T NO KINDA ANIMAL SHE EVER SEEN BEFORE."
"...AND THE *SOUND* IT MADE!"
rrrrRRRRRRROOOOOOOWWWW

RRROOOOOOWWLLL

OH MY *GOD*, LOUIS!!

IT'S JUST ALLEY CATS! SAME AS EVERY NIGHT!

THEN WHAT HAPPENED?!

KEEP GOING!

ONE-EYED TOM GOT *THIIIS* CLOSE TO GRAN...

...THEN SHE HOOFED IT!

RAN TO HER CAR, TURNED AROUND, AND FOUND MAIN STREET!

DIDN'T LOOK BACK.

WH–

AND THAT'S THE FIRST TIME ANYONE SAW HIM! GET HOME SAFE, LOU!

PROMISE?!
NEXT TIME WE HANG OUT?

NEXT TIME.
SURE.
I PROMISE!

OKAY, WELL, I'M GOING HOME NOW...
...AT NIGHT...
...IN THE DARK...
G'NIGHT!

MAMA! THIS IS LOU!
HI...SNAP'S MOM.

LATER, LOU!
LATER, SNAP!

DON'T RUN INTO ANY MONSTERRRS!

WHAT?

WHAAAAT?!

THAT'S IT, LET 'EM EAT AT THEIR OWN PACE.
DON'T LET ANY GET IN THEIR NOSE.
THEY'RE NEARLY READY TO EAT ON THEIR OWN.

HOW D'YOU KNOW ALL THIS STUFF?
I GOT LICENSED AS A REHABILITATOR, FEW YEARS BACK.

HEH.
I AIN'T GOT A LICENSE. IS IT ***ILLEGAL*** FOR ME TO DO THIS?

YEAH.

WAIT. ***REALLY?***
DON'T WORRY ABOUT IT. I'M SUPERVISING.

YOU–
–YOU AIN'T EVEN WATCHING!

I'M NOT LICENSED ANYMORE. MY PERMIT EXPIRED YEARS AGO.

WH–I DON'T WANT TO KILL THESE BABIES!!
YOU WON'T.
BUT–
I WATCHED YOU FEED THE OTHERS. YOU DID A FINE JOB.
BELIEVE ME, I'D TELL YA IF YA DIDN'T.

...OKAY.

SO...

...WHATCHA DOIN'?

PUTTIN' THE SPINE OF THIS RABBIT TOGETHER.

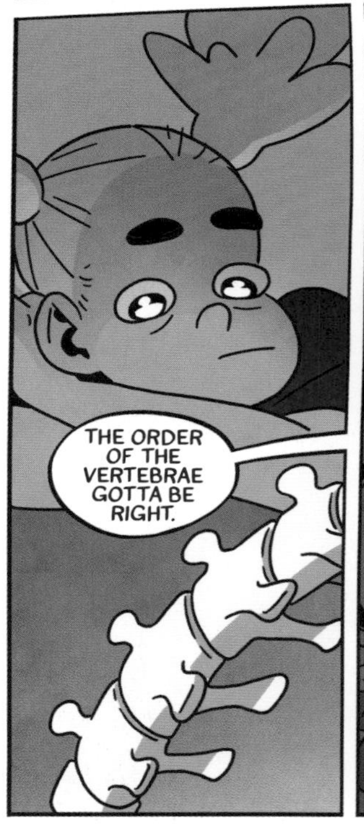
THE ORDER OF THE VERTEBRAE GOTTA BE RIGHT.

JACKS, IF YOU CARE ABOUT ANIMALS...
...HOW COME YOU MESS AROUND WITH THEIR BONES?

"MESS AROUND"?
WELL, Y'KNOW...

I AIN'T DISRESPECTIN' THESE CRITTERS.
"CRITTERS DIE ALL THE TIME, BUT IT OUGHT TO BE FOR A ***REASON.***"
"THAT'S WHAT EVEN THE ***LEAST*** OF US DESERVE."
"BUT ROADKILL'S A LOUSY WAY TO END UP."
THUD
"LOTSA FOLKS DON'T EVEN NOTICE WHEN THEY HIT SOMETHIN'."
"SO I NOTICE 'EM."

I–
–TO GET THEIR LITTLE SPIRITS TO MOVE ALONG.
THEN PUT 'EM WHERE THE BUGGIES CAN SAFELY EAT 'EM UP.
THEN, THEY BECOME SOMETHING NEW.
AND THEY'RE REMEMBERED.

I'VE GOT AN IDEA!
OH?

ONE SEC!

ALL YOUR SKELETONS WERE JUST KINDA *SITTIN'.*
shake
shake
shake

BUT I GOT ALL THESE ANIMAL MAGAZINES WITH COOL, ACTIONY POSES!!
SEE?
WHAT IF YOU MADE THE RABBIT LOOK LIKE IT WAS JUMPING OR SOMETHING?
ANIMALS

MMM, INTERESTING...

I'VE ALWAYS USED THE SAME POSES, THOUGH...
I COULD HELP!

YOU **REALLY** DO LIKE ALL THIS STUFF?
I GUESS SO.
I REALLY LIKE ANIMALS.
I NEVER THOUGHT OF LEARNIN' ABOUT 'EM THIS WAY.

OKAY, THEN.
WE'LL TRY IT.

"FIND A GOOD POSE WE CAN USE."
LIKE... **ACTUAL** BONES?
LIKE, FROM AN ANIMAL?

YES. AN ACTUAL ANIMAL.
WHY?
'CAUSE IT'S INTERESTING.

WE'RE FULL OF SKELETONS, LOUIS.
HAHA!
YOU'RE SO WEIRD.
ANIMAL

PSH. SAYS YOU!

HEY! YOU WANT ME TO DO YOURS?
BLECH! NO!

...FIIINE. YOU CAN DO MY TOES.

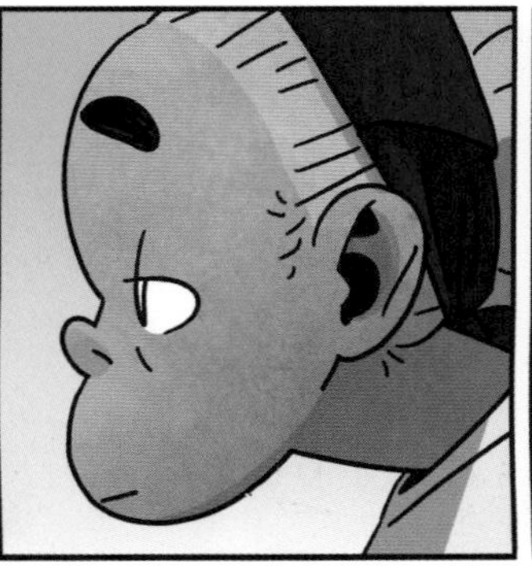

Y'KNOW, LOU...

IF YOU WANTED A *GIRLY-GIRL* FRIEND YOU SHOULDA PICKED LIKE...

...***LITERALLY*** ANY OTHER GIRL AT OUR SCHOOL.

NAW, I DON'T CARE IF YOU DON'T LIKE GIRLY THINGS.

YOU DON'T MAKE FUN OF **ME** FOR LIKING THEM.

OH!

SPEAKING OF WHY WE'RE FRIENDS...

CHECK IT!

DIRECTOR'S CUT

WITCH'S HILL

The Last Door

KNOC KNOCK!

WHAAAT!!

THE DIRECTOR'S CUT OF WITCH'S HILL FIVE?!

HMMM...
YUCK!
YOU'RE *LITTLE* BABIES!
HOW DO YOU *POOP* SO MUCH?
BLECH!
SPLURCH

THERE!

GOOD 'N' CLEAN!

YOU'RE GONNA FILL IT WITH **POOP** AGAIN, AREN'T YOU?

YES!
I!
AM!

I LOVE THEM!
DON'T GET ATTACHED.
YEAH, I KNOW.

SO WHAT CAN I DO?!
ONCE I BEND THE SPINE INTO THE RIGHT SHAPE, YOU CAN HELP SORT THE TOE BONES.

...

...

...

WHATCHU STARING AT, GIRL?
OH! UH, NOTHIN'...
OH? YOU AIN'T STARIN' AT MY EYEPATCH?
WELL, I GUESS I WAS SORTA WONDERIN' ABOUT IT...
SO ASK.

YOU GOT AN EYE UNDER THERE?
NO.

tap
A FOX ATE IT.

FINE, DON'T TELL ME!

IT WAS A MOTORCYCLE ACCIDENT.

DECADES AGO.

YOU USED TO RIDE A MOTORCYCLE!?
I USED TO ***RACE*** THEM.

WHAT!!

TELL ME ***EVERYTHING!***
WHEN?
DID YOU WIN?
WHAT KIND OF MOTOR-CYCLE?
WHERE DID YOU RACE?
WAS IT DANGEROUS?
DO YOU STILL RIDE THEM?

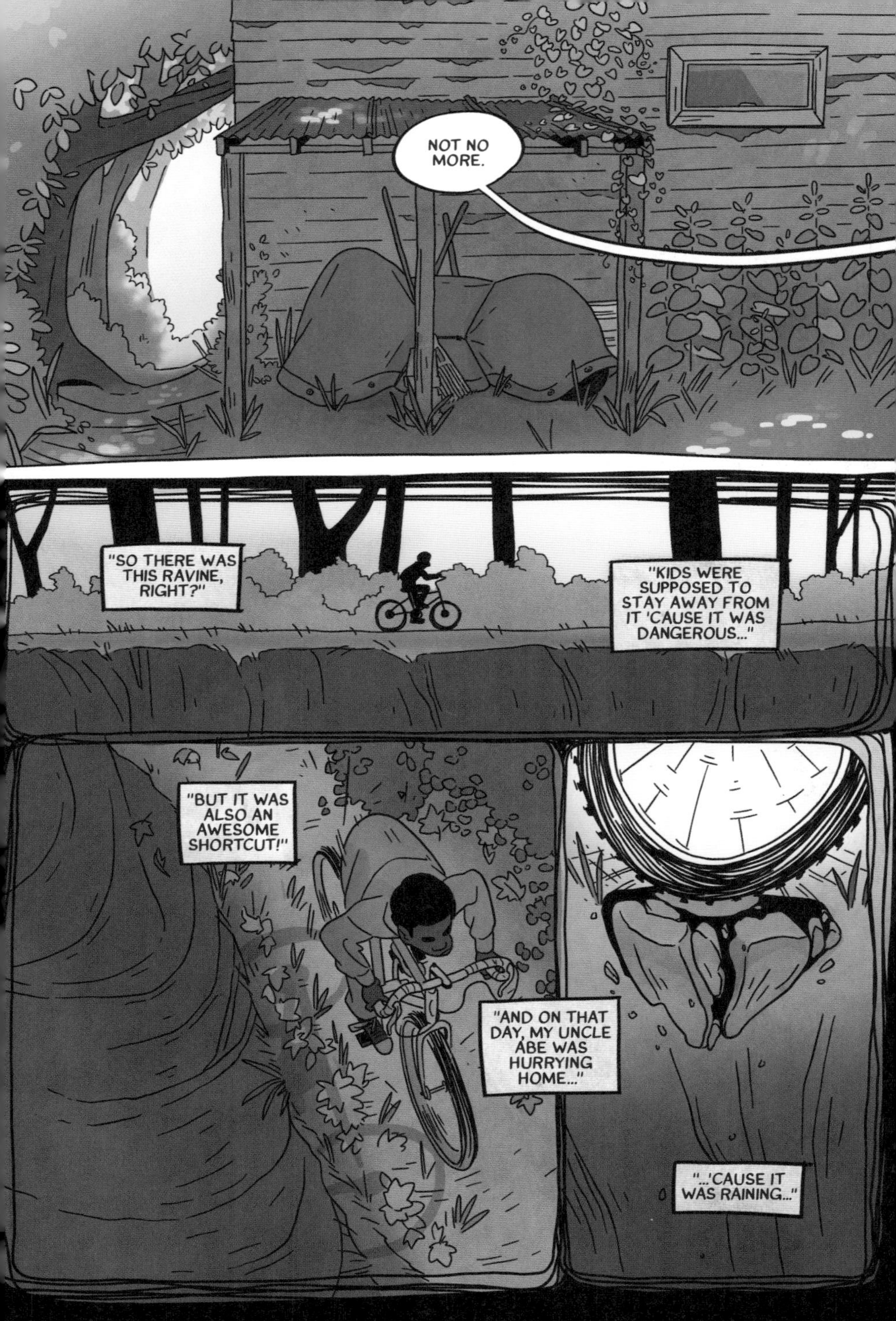
NOT NO MORE.
"SO THERE WAS THIS RAVINE, RIGHT?"
"KIDS WERE SUPPOSED TO STAY AWAY FROM IT 'CAUSE IT WAS DANGEROUS..."
"BUT IT WAS ALSO AN AWESOME SHORTCUT!"
"AND ON THAT DAY, MY UNCLE ABE WAS HURRYING HOME..."
"...'CAUSE IT WAS RAINING..."

CRASH!
"AND HE MUST HAVE HIT HIS HEAD WHEN HE FELL, 'CAUSE WHEN HE WOKE UP—"
"—TIME HAD PASSED."

"HE HAD A TWISTED ANKLE..."
"...AND WAS ABOUT TO CALL FOR HELP..."
"...WHEN HE HEARD IT."
RRRRROOOOOOWWWLLL
"HE TRIED TO CLIMB OUT, BUT HIS ANKLE THROBBED."
"AND THE RAIN HAD TURNED THE STEEP WALLS TO MUD..."
"...AND THAT'S WHEN HE FINALLY SAW IT!"

"CLIMBING!"
"DOWN!"
"THE RAVINE!"
"RIGHT TOWARD HIM!"
"THEN ITS MOUTH OPENED..."
"...AND OPENED..."
"...AND OPENED!"

"BUT THEN!"
ABE!
"IT HAD GOT SO LATE, MY GRAN WENT LOOKIN' FOR 'IM."
"AND WHEN ABE LOOKED AGAIN..."
"...THE CREATURE WAS GONE!"
"VANISHED!"
"GRANNY HAULED HIM OUTTA THAT RAVINE HERSELF."
WHOA, SO YOUR UNCLE GOT A GOOD LOOK AT IT, HUH?
HE SAID IT GOT REAL CLOSE!

SO LIKE... HAVE *YOU* EVER SEEN ONE-EYED TOM?
NOT *YET,* BUT I–

COOL ***SHIRT!***
REALLY?

YEAH! I ***LOVE*** DRAGONS, DUDE!
"DRAGON" IS IN MY FRICKIN' ***NAME!***
OH, YEAH.
WELL, THE SHIRT'S PRETTY OLD.
I GET ***BOTH*** MY BROTHERS' HAND-ME-DOWNS.

YOU CAN TOTALLY HAVE IT.

REALLY!?

UH, YEAH, LIKE I SAID, IT'S A HANDED-DOWN HAND-ME-DOWN.

...CAN WE DO OUR HOMEWORK NOW?

LET'S TRADE.

SHE WON'T EVEN NOTICE!

CAREFUL!
'80's
old family
creeeeee
WHOA!
SNAP!
CRAP!
SNAP?
GOT IT!

SHOVE

HAH

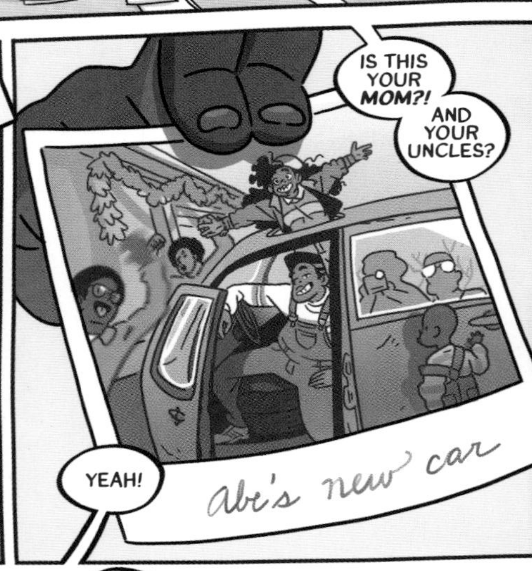
IS THIS YOUR *MOM?!*
AND YOUR UNCLES?
YEAH!
abe's new car

WE GOT ALL THESE WHEN WE HELPED MY GRAN MOVE FROM HER OLD HOUSE.

I'M GONNA TRY THIS ON!

HEEHEE HEHE!
HA!
HAHA!
ARK ARK
ck clack

HEY, MAMA!
HOW WAS TRAINING?
LOOK AT THE SHIRT LOU GAVE ME!
WE DID A SWAP!
MM-HMM, THAT'S NICE, BABY.

WE'RE DOIN' OUR HOMEWORK! CAN LOU STAY FOR DINNER?

IF IT'S OKAY WITH HIS PARENTS.
FLOP!

THINK YOU CAN HANDLE DINNER TONIGHT, BABY?
YEAH!

THAT MEANS MAC 'N' CHEESE!

THAT MY SKIRT?

SNAP GIVE IT TO YOU?
YES, MA'AM. SHE, UH, SAID YOU WOULDN'T MIND...
YOU NEVER WEAR THAT ONE, MAMA!
SIGH. SHE AIN'T WRONG. IT'S ALL YOURS, KID...
...YOUR PARENTS MIND YOU HAVIN' IT, THOUGH?
...DUNNO.

WELL, IF THEY DO YOU CAN TELL 'EM I LET YOU HAVE IT—
—WHAT WE GOT FOR VEGGIES, KID?
GREEN BEANS!?
YOU LIKE GREEN BEANS?
NOD

HA HA!
HA HAHA
I WASN'T EXPECTIN' YOU TODAY.

I DIDN'T RECOGNIZE HER 'CAUSE SHE'S SO YOUNG, BUT...

...THAT'S MY GRANNY!

THAT'S *YOU* AND MY GRANNY, AIN'T IT?

HUH.

I HAD WONDERED...

...BECAUSE OF YOUR NAME...

Y'KNOW YOU LOOK LIKE HER SOMETIMES?

MAYBE NOT RIGHT NOW...

DID YOU KNOW I WAS HER GRAND-DAUGHTER WHEN YOU MET ME!?
DID MY GRAN USED TO RIDE *MOTOR-CYCLES!?!*

ARE YOU STILL FRIENDS?

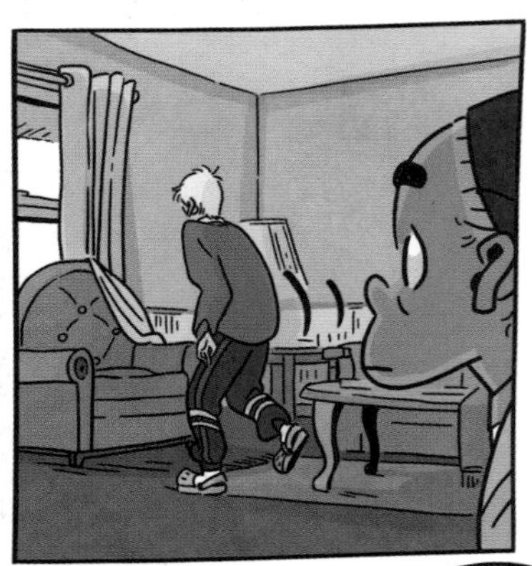

FOR ALL THE FAMILIES FOR YOU TO BE A PART OF...

YOU'RE PART OF *HERS...*
HOW DID YOU KNOW HER?

IT'S AN *OLD* STORY.
I WANNA KNOW!
IT'S A *LONG* STORY.
PLEASE!
SIGH
I TOLD YA I USED TO RACE MOTOR-CYCLES?
WELL...
"IT WAS *AT* ONE OF THOSE RACES I MET YOUR GRAN FOR THE FIRST TIME."
"IT WAS ONE OF THE...*LESS OFFICIAL* RACES..."

"WE WEREN'T A PICKY BUNCH."
"THE 'WHERE' AND THE 'WHO' DIDN'T MATTER ALL THAT MUCH."
"THE TRACK WAS WHATEVER STRETCH OF DIRT WE COULD FIND THAT WAS LONG ENOUGH."
"AND HECK, ANYONE FOOL ENOUGH TO PARTICIPATE WAS WELCOME!"

"THEY DIDN'T MUCH MIND A WOMAN RACIN' WITH 'EM..."
FINISH
"...WEREN'T CRAZY ABOUT US *WINNIN'* THOUGH!"
"—*BUT!* I WAS TALL, GANGLY, COVERED IN DIRT, AND IF I DIDN'T TALK MUCH...
EVERYONE JUST ASSUMED I WAS A FELLA."
"EVERYONE *EXCEPT*—"
LOOKS LIKE YOU GOT *NICKED* THERE, HONEY!

ON YOUR CHEEK, RIGHT HERE.

I COULD TELL YOU WERE A HANDSOME ONE!

THANK YA, MA'AM, BUT I'M NOT...
I'M ACTUALLY A WO—
MAKES NO DIFFERENCE TO ME!

I STAND BY WHAT I SAID!
M-MA'AM! YOUR KERCHIEF!
KEEP IT, HONEY!
JESSIE, GIRL, YOU *SHAMELESS!*

WAIT!

ALLOW ME...
ALLOW ME TO RETURN IT TO YOU!

KNOCK
KNOCK

CREEE

JACKS!
HELLO MISS JESSAMINE

OH! AH...
...THESE ARE FOR YOU, MA'AM!

VIOLETS.
AW, *THANK YA,* HONEY, TRULY.
BUT I'M–

AH– AH– AH–

CHOO!

–AFRAID I'M TERRIBLY ALLERGIC TO FLOWERS.

OH! I DIDN'T...

I'M REAL SORRY!

IT'S FINE, HONEY, YOU–

...
PFT
YOU—
HA HA HA
—YOU HUCKED 'EM INTO THE **SUN!**
HA
"AND THAT WAS IT."
"THAT WAS THE MOMENT I FELL FOR HER..."
"...WELL, **ONE** OF THEM, ANYWAYS."

"LOTTA FOLKS SAW US TWO TOGETHER AS ALL KINDS OF WRONG..."
"...SO WE HAD TO MAKE THE MOST OF IT!"
"AND SOME GOOD FOLKS STILL SAW US AS NEIGHBORS."
"I COULDA STAYED LIKE THAT, WITH JESSAMINE, FOREVER."
"WE WERE HAPPY."
"BUT THERE WAS ONE THING..."
IT JUST AIN'T FAIR!
HONK
MY FAMILY GOT ONE TRADITION:
NAMIN' OUR BABY GIRLS AFTER OUR FAVORITE FLOWERS.
SHOULD BE THE SIMPLEST THING IN THE WORLD, HM?
I AIN'T EVER LIKED A FLOWER MY WHOLE LIFE!
SO WHAT AM I SUPPOSED TO DO...

ALLS I CAN DO IS HOPE AN' PRAY FOR BOYS!

"...JESSAMINE WANTED A FAMILY."

A **BIG, SPRAWLING** *FAMILY!*
SPILLIN' OUTTA EVERY ROOM!
"SHE'D IMAGINE THE HOLIDAYS, THE BIG SUNDAY DINNERS...THE PITTER-PATTER OF LITTLE FEET..."
"SHE WANTED A BUSTLIN' HOME..."

"BUT I... DIDN'T."

"IT DIDN'T MATTER AT FIRST..."
"WE LOVED EACH OTHER."

"BUT AFTER TIME...OUR FEELINGS DIDN'T CHANGE."

WE WOULDN'T EVEN BE THE ONLY... *UNCONVENTIONAL* FAMILY!
THAT WIDOWER NEXT TOWN OVER'S RAISIN' HIS LOT WITH ANOTHER FELLA...
AN'...AN' THAT COUPLE IN VIRGINIA, THE LOVINGS, THEY—
THAT'S NOT WHY I DON'T WANT KIDS, JESSIE...

"'I'M AFRAID I'LL TURN OUT LIKE MY PARENTS.'"

YOUR PARENTS WERE **AWFUL**, JACKS, WORSE THAN AWFUL, BUT YOU WOULDN'T **BE** LIKE THEM!
I BET THEY THOUGHT THEY'D BE GREAT PARENTS...
...BET THEY **NEVER** THOUGHT THEY'D **THROW OUT** THEIR OWN KID.
NO, YOU'D **NEVER** DO WHAT THEY DID!

I JUST CAN'T TAKE THAT CHANCE, JESSIE...

I **WON'T**.

...I'M SORRY.

...ME, TOO.

"AND THAT WAS IT."

"JESSAMINE MET A KIND MAN AND THEY RAISED THE FAMILY SHE WANTED."
"SHE GOT WHAT SHE WANTED..."

"...AND I SUPPOSE I DID AS WELL."

EXHALE

WH–
sniff

THAT'S **SO SAD,** JACKS!

HERE.
RUB RUB

IT WAS A LONG TIME AGO.
BUT YOU **LOVED** EACH OTHER!

YES, WELL...

IF WE'D STAYED TOGETHER, YOU WOULDN'T EXIST.

AND THAT'D BE A SHAME.

HEM

SINCE YOU'RE HERE, I MAY AS WELL GIVE YOU SOMETHING I BEEN MEANIN' TO...
wsh wsh wsh

AND THEN SHE GAVE ME THIS!

IT'S GOT ALL THE BONES AND HOW THEY GO TOGETHER!
JACKS DREW IT ALL HERSELF!
SO IT'S *ONE OF A KIND*...
...BUT JACKS SAID I COULD USE IT TO FAMILIARIZE MYSELF WITH BONES!
HMM...
YUP!
STILL CREEPY!
CREEK MIDDLE SCHOOL
AW, C'MON, LULU! IT'S ***COOL!***
HEY!

HAHAHA
HAHAHAH
WHAT. IS. YOUR. PROBLEM?!
THIS IS, LIKE, AN ANTIQUE!
HEY!
GIVE IT BACK!

OH! HAHA! YOU'RE EVEN CREEPIER THAN I THOUGHT, SNOTTY!
GIVE IT BACK!
SO CLOSE!
HA HA HAHA HA
TRIP
AH!

THANKS, LULU!
YUP!
HEY, LOUIS!

WHAT GIVES?
YOU USED TO BE SORTA COOL BEFORE YOU CAUGHT FREAK FROM THIS ONE!
IT'S LULU. AND SNAP'S COOLER THAN YOU ARE, TRAVIS.
REALLY?! 'CAUSE SHE GOT YOU WEARING SKIRTS AND NAIL POLISH...

HA!
WHAT'D SHE DO?
NUDGE

SHE STEAL YOUR—

OOF!
ARE YOU MAD, MAMA?

I DON'T WANT ANY MORE CALLS LIKE THIS, SNAPDRAGON.

SIGH
BUT IF IT'S GOT TO BE FOR ANY REASON... I SUPPOSE YOU COULD DO ***WORSE*** THAN HEAD-BUTTING A ***BULLY.***

...

BABY, YOU KNOW YOU CAN TALK TO ME 'BOUT ANYTHING... RIGHT?
YEAH?

NO, MAMA.

YOU CAN TALK TO ME ABOUT THESE THINGS—

I'M JUST... I'M NOT *LIKE* OTHER GIRLS!

I *WONDERED* IF MAYBE I WAS REALLY A BOY, LIKE LULU'S A GIRL...BUT THAT DON'T FEEL RIGHT, *EITHER*...

LET'S GET ONE THING STRAIGHT.

YOU STOOD UP FOR YOURSELF, AND YOUR FRIEND, AGAINST A *BULLY*–
–SO YOU ACT *JUST FINE.*
I'M *PROUD* OF WHO YOU ARE, BABY–
–AND I DON'T WANT YOU ACTIN' ANY OTHER WAY.
GOT IT?

GOT IT.

NOW, WE GOIN' BACK TO THE *STATION* CAUSE I HAD MY TRAININ' INTERRUPTED BY *SOMEBODY...*
YEAH, I *THOUGHT* YOU'D LIKE THAT...

HEY, MAMÁ?
MM-HM?

...DID GRAN EVER TALK WITH YOU 'BOUT...THIS KIND OF STUFF?

SHE DID, ACTUALLY.

HAD TALKS WITH MY BROTHERS AN' ME 'BOUT ALL SORTS OF STUFF THEY BE CALLIN' "PROGRESSIVE" THESE DAYS.

YOUR GRAN'S ALWAYS BEEN AHEAD OF HER TIME. YOU'D BE SURPRISED!

...

WHY DO YOU ASK?

...NO REASON.

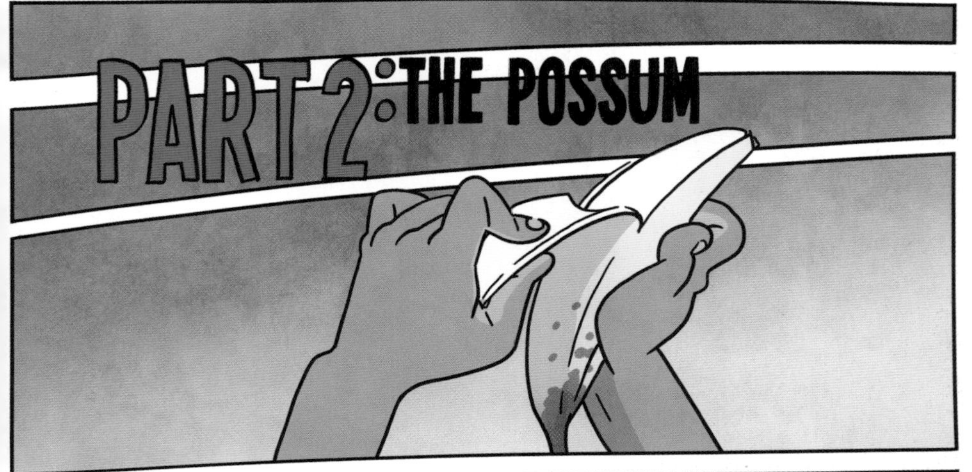
PART 2: THE POSSUM

smk smk smk

AAAW, ARE YOU FEELING LEFT OUT, GEEBIES?
smk smk smk smk smk

HERE YOU GO!

READY?
Haha ha haha
blch

I CAN'T BELIEVE IT'S ALREADY TIME...
I'M GONNA MISS 'EM...

NOW, WHAT'S THAT FACE?

I TOLD YOU NOT TO GET ATTACHED.
IT'S NOT THAT.

SO WHERE WE TAKIN' THEM?

THE WOODS.
SIGH

TUMP
THIS SPOT'LL DO.

ALL RIGHT, LITTLE BUDDIES...

...OFF YOU GO!

HEY, JACKS?
NOW THAT THE POSSUMS ARE FREE...
...AND I DON'T NEED YOUR HELP WITH 'EM ANYMORE...

WHAT ABOUT THE OTHER STUFF?
EH?

"I MEAN, CAN I STILL HELP WITH ALL THE SKELETON STUFF?"
LEFT
RIG

...IF... Y'KNOW...YOU STILL **WANT** MY HELP...
IF YOU LIKE.

REALLY?!
YEAH, THE EXTRA HELP HAS BEEN GOOD.
TUMP! TUMP!

YER DOIN' A GOOD JOB.

NOW!
USE THEM SKINNY ARMS AND GET THIS LAST STUBBORN LITTLE JOEY OUT HERE!
HAH HAH!
ck ck ck
AHA!
THE REAL REASON YER KEEPIN' ME AROUND!

YA CAUGHT ME.
HA, C'MON LITTLE BABY, TIME TO GO!

NUDGE

UH.

UH?

UH?!
WHAT *IS* I—

OH.
YOU CAN SEE HER, HUH?

YEEEP, GHOSTS IS REAL.
I BEEN SAYIN' AS MUCH.
THE DAY YOU BRUNG THEM BABIES TO ME...
...YOU CARRIED MAMA HERE, *TOO.*
I KNOW YOU'RE NOT A WITCH.
OH?
MAMAS SOMETIMES STICK AROUND FOR THEIR BABIES.
LEFTOVER INSTINCTS, I IMAGINE.
WAIT—

—DOES THAT MEAN YOU REALLY **ARE** A WITCH?!?!

YEAH.

WHAT!?

SO IF WITCHES AND GHOSTS ARE REAL...

...WHAT ABOUT VAMPIRES?

ZOMBIES?

WERE-WOLVES?!

GASP!

DRAGONS!?!?

ARE DRAGONS REAL?!?

CAN YOU TURN PEOPLE INTO THINGS?

CAN *YOU* TURN INTO THINGS?

. . .

OH! CAN YOU *FLY?!*

WHAT SPELLS CAN YOU CAST?

DO YOU HAVE A FAMILIAR?

A CAULDRON?

A WAND?

A BROOM?

I IMAGINE YOU GOT A PICTURE IN YOUR HEAD OF WHAT WITCHES IS.
LIKE FROM THOSE MOVIES YOU WATCH.
EVIL, UGLY, SCARY THINGS...

WELL, IT AIN'T LIKE THAT.

IT AIN'T EXCITIN'.
IT'S HARD, LONELY WORK.

WITCHES DON'T FIT INTO THE ROLES WE'RE ***SUPPOSED*** TO.
SO WE'RE ALWAYS ON THE OUTSIDE.

AND SO, WITCHES GOT MADE INTO SCARY THINGS TO BE FEARED.
TO EXCUSE THE CRUEL THINGS DONE TO US.
THAT'S WHAT SCARED FOLKS ***DID***. ***STILL*** DO.

DO YOU UNDERSTAND?

YEAH.
HEY, JACKS?

COULD I BE A WITCH?
WOULD YOU...
... I DON'T KNOW HOW IT WORKS...
...WOULD YOU TEACH ME?
SNAP.
NOT EVERYONE IS ABLE TO USE MAGIC...

AND LIKE I WAS SAYIN', IT AIN'T LIKE MOVIES AND STORIES.
I CAN'T MAKE YOU ANY PROMISES...
SO YOU'LL DO IT? YOU'LL TEACH ME?!
NOW, YOU GOTTA LISTEN TO ME, ALL RIGHT?
OKAY!
IT'S IMPORTANT TO DO THIS A CERTAIN WAY, UNDERSTAND?
YEAH!!

WELL, ALL RIGHT, THEN.
APPRENTICE.
KNOCK! KNOCK! KNOCK!!
LUUU!
HI, MRS. HILL!
HELLO, SNAP.

LU!
I GOTTA TELL YOU SOMETHING AWESOME!

OH. YOU TWO ARE HERE...
HEH HEH.
WH— HEY! WHY WOULDN'T WE BE?!?

C'MON. LET'S GO TO THE ROOF.

'KAY!
ZIP!!
ARGH!!
HEY!!

YEAH! TAKE YOUR WEIRDO SQUIRREL GIRLFRIEND AND STAY OUT THERE, LULU!
BLEH!

SNAP! WHAT'S UP?
tap tap tap

MAGIC IS REAL, I CAN SEE GHOSTS,
JACKS IS A WITCH, AND I'M GONNA BE ONE, TOO!
...UH-HUH.
I'M BEING SERIOUS!
UH-HUH.
REALLY!
C'MON, SNAP, DON'T TEASE ME.
NO! NO! I'M NOT—
—I SWEAR, IT'S TRUE!
BUT THAT AIN'T THE ONLY THING I LEARNED...
DO I GET A WAND OR A HAT OR A FAMILIAR OR A BROOM—
NAW.
YOU DON'T NEED ANY OF THAT HOCUS-POCUS.
AWW.

SOMETHING THE MATTER?
NO! NO! SORRY!
THAT JUNK'LL CLUTTER YOUR BRAIN AND DISTRACT YOU FROM REAL CONTROL.
YOU GOTTA BE ABLE TO RELY ON YOURSELF.
'CAUSE MAGIC'S ALL ABOUT YOUR OWN WILL AND ENERGY.
AND THE GHOSTS?
GHOSTS IS JUST LEFTOVER ENERGY.
YOU CAN ALREADY SEE IT—THAT'S GOOD.
A GOOD FIRST STEP...
...BUT CONNECTIN' WITH IT AND USIN' IT HOW YOU WISH...
...THAT'S THE FINICKY BIT—
—THAT'S MAGIC.

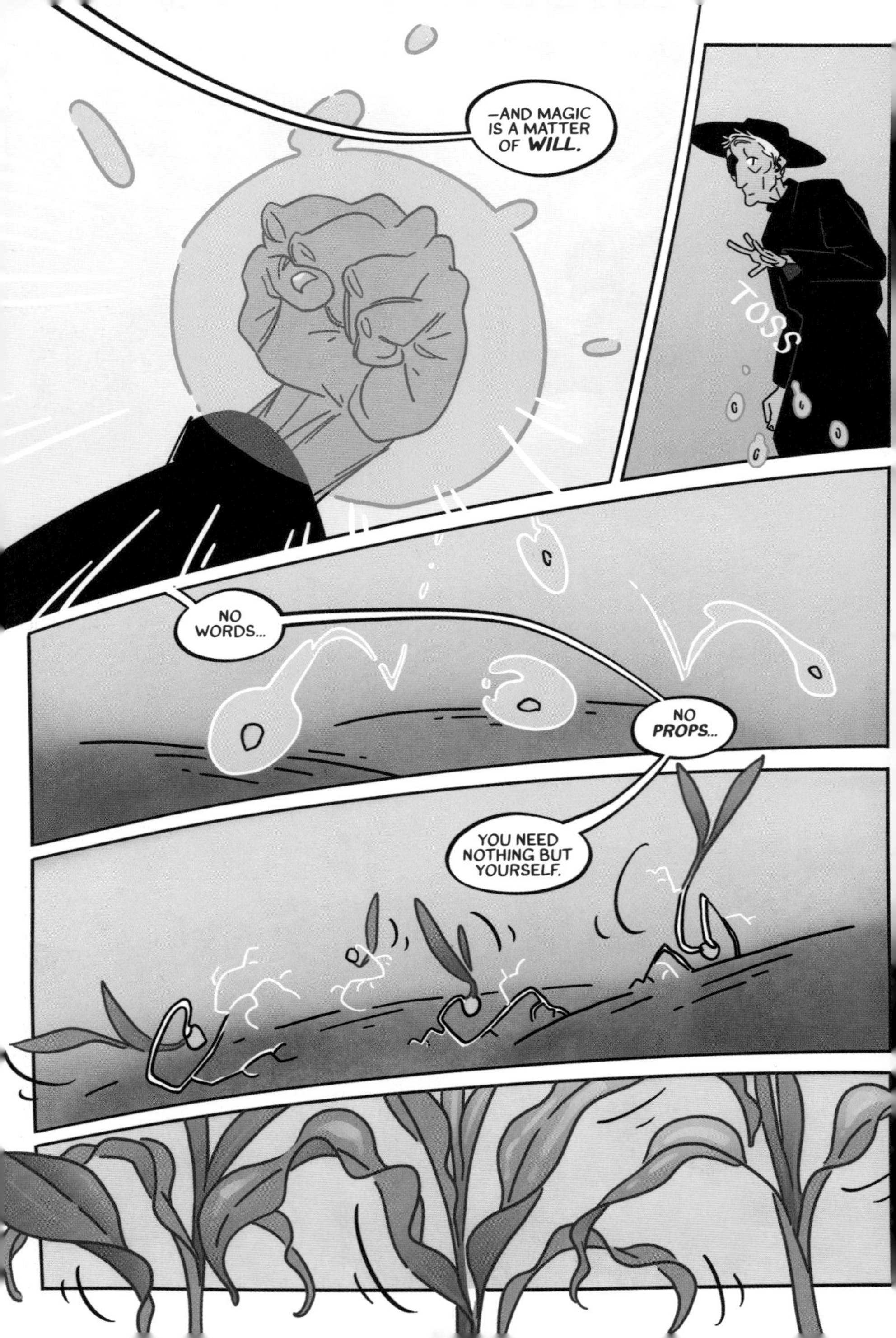
—AND MAGIC IS A MATTER OF WILL.
TOSS
NO WORDS...
NO PROPS...
YOU NEED NOTHING BUT YOURSELF.

WHOA...

SO...WE ALL GOT GHOSTS IN US...
...AND I GOTTA USE **MY** GHOST TO DO STUFF WITH, LIKE...
...**OTHER** GHOSTS?

WELL, THAT'S...
...I MEAN...
...**TECHNICALLY** RIGHT...
THAT IS **SO COOL!**

HOW DO I—
GRK!!

UUUH...
YOU... WHAT?
WHAT IS IT?
OH, THAT'S JUST—
BUCK! SCRAM!
SCRAM!

THAT'S JUST *BUCK.*
MOST GHOSTS DON'T LINGER PAST A FEW MONTHS. TOPS.
SNRT

"A FEW YEARS AGO, I FOUND 'IM BARELY ALIVE."
"I STAYED WITH 'IM 'TIL HE PASSED."
"BUT HE'S A STUBBORN ONE...."
"...AND NOW HE JUST *WON'T LEAVE!*"

HAHA HA
SNF
SNF

GASP!

JACKS!
A FOX!
SHOVE

IT'S THE SAME ONE I SAW BEFORE!

I CAN TELL 'CAUSE IT'S GOT ONLY...

...ONE...

...GREEN...

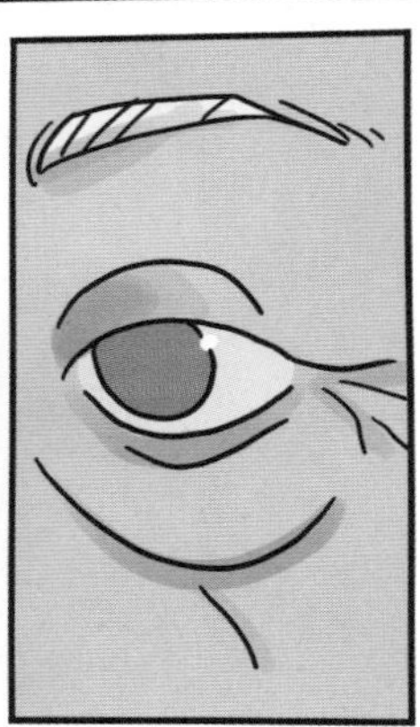

EYYYEEEEEEE!!!
HOLY CRAP DOES THAT FOX HAVE ***YOUR*** ***EYE?!?!***

MM-HM. TOLD YOU A FOX ATE MY EYE.

WELL. I ***FED*** 'IM MY EYE. IF I'M BEIN' PRECISE.

"IT WAS MY FAULT FOR DRIVIN' EMOTIONAL."

SSCCCCCCRREEEEEEEEEEEEEEEEEEEEEEEEEEEEEE-

"SHOULDN'TA BEEN DRIVIN' THAT NIGHT."

"I HIT A FOX..."

"...AND I'D BLINDED THE POOR THING."

"AND I... COULDN'T HANDLE THAT..."

"AND IT WORKED!"
"BUT IT WAS A SPUR OF THE MOMENT SPELL, AND WELL..."

...I MAY HAVE... *CURSED* HIM.
BY MISTAKE.

"WE'D BECOME LINKED."

IN FACT, HE'D EVEN CHECK IN ON JESSAMINE ONCE
HOLD IT.
WHOA WHOA WHOA.

ARE YOU TELLING ME—
ONE-EYED TOM IS A **REAL**, DECADES-OLD FOX—
—AND THE OLD LADY YOU PUT SKELETONS TOGETHER WITH **SHARES AN EYE WITH HIM?!**
YEAH.
TURNS OUT TOM WASN'T HAUNTING US, AFTER ALL.
JUST WATCHING OVER US.

"...OR WATCHING OVER MY UNCLE WHEN HE FELL IN A RAVINE."
ROOOOOWLL!
"AND MAKING NOISE TO LEAD MY GRAN TO HIM..."

WOW.

YEAH.

HEY!

DO YOU THINK THERE WERE OTHER TIMES, TOO?

HM?

LIKE, OTHER TIMES HE HELPED OUT YOUR FAMILY THAT YOU DON'T KNOW ABOUT?
HUH.
...I SUPPOSE...

A FEW MONTHS AGO...
"I WOULDN'T KNOW, WOULD I?"

—HOW MANY TIMES DO YOU NEED TO HEAR IT?!
WE'RE *THROUGH,* CHUCK!

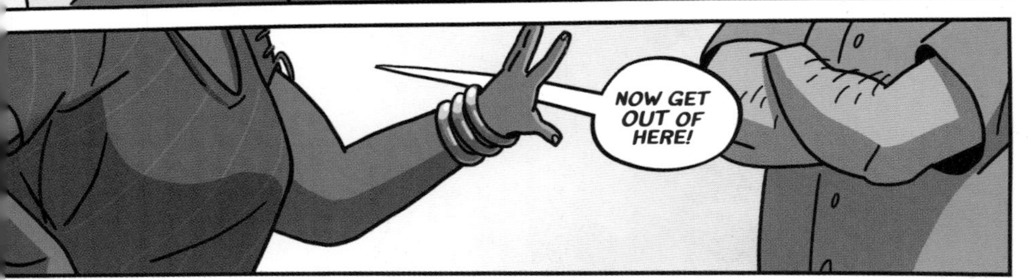
NOW GET OUT OF HERE!

IF YOU'RE GONNA BE LIKE THIS I'M TAKING MY DAMN DOG BACK!
OH NO YOU ARE NOT.
AND IF I CATCH YOU SKULKING AROUND MY HOUSE AGAIN—
—OR ANYWHERE NEAR MY DAUGHTER OR HER DOG...
NOW GET OUT OF HERE!

. . .
NO.
I'M NOT
LEAVING
WITHO—

yaaaaawaaawwnn
fumble fumble
scratch scratch
SLAM
SQUEEE

BACK TO THE PRESENT...

yaaaaaawwww...
shuffle
shuffle

KNOCK
KNOCK
?

MORNIN', JACKS!
YOU KNOW WHAT *TIME* IT IS, GIRL?
HEH, SORRY!

I KNOW IT'S *EARLY* BUT I COULDN'T WAIT!

I'M READY TO START *WITCH TRAINING!*

CLAP
SNRT!

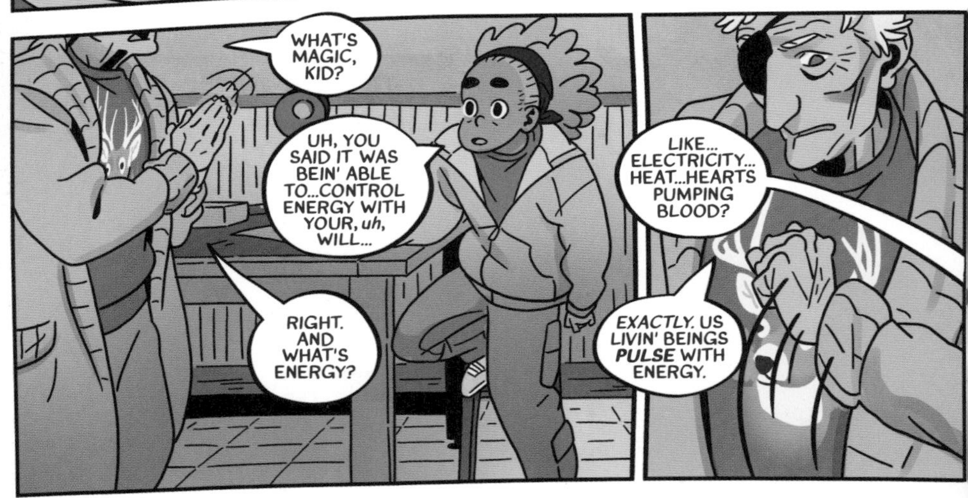
WHAT'S MAGIC, KID?
UH, YOU SAID IT WAS BEIN' ABLE TO...CONTROL ENERGY WITH YOUR, *uh*, WILL...
RIGHT. AND WHAT'S ENERGY?
LIKE... ELECTRICITY... HEAT...HEARTS PUMPING BLOOD?
EXACTLY. US LIVIN' BEINGS ***PULSE*** WITH ENERGY.

YOU GOTTA LEARN HOW TO TAP INTO IT...
...MANIPULATE IT...
...THEN YOU CAN DO ALL SORTS OF THINGS.
YEAH?! LIKE WHAT?!

EH, WE'LL GET TO THAT WHEN WE GET TO IT.
AW, C'MON!
CAN YOU FLY?!

FLYING WOULD BE *FRIVOLOUS.*

"THERE ARE BETTER USES FOR MAGIC THAN THAT."

WAKE UP!!

SEE 'IM?
YEAH!

SEE IF YOU CAN'T REACH OUT TO 'IM.
CLOSE YOUR EYES.
CONCENTRATE.

TRY WARMIN' YOUR HANDS.

FOCUS ON THE WARMTH OF YOUR PALMS...

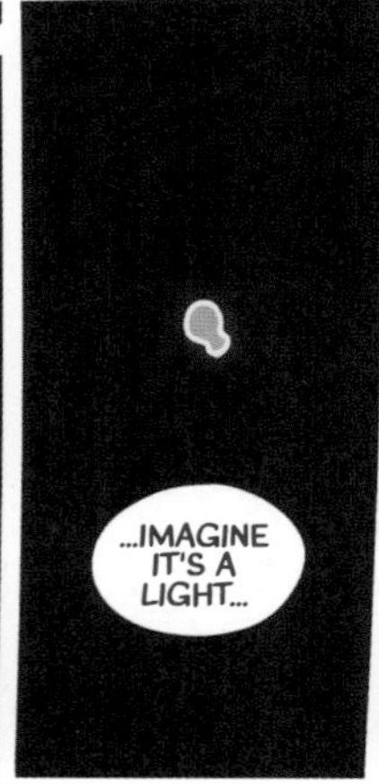
...IMAGINE IT'S A LIGHT...

...FEEL YOUR HEARTBEAT...
...NO, DON'T HOLD YOUR BREATH.

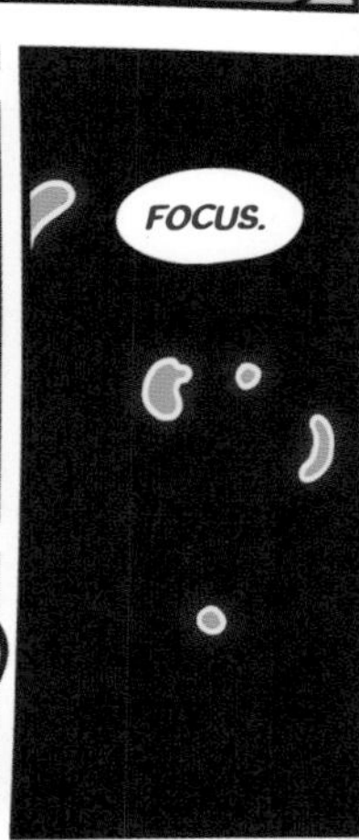
FOCUS.

NOW TRY...

...IT DIDN'T WORK...
DON'T FRET.

IT DON'T ALWAYS CLICK RIGHT AWAY.
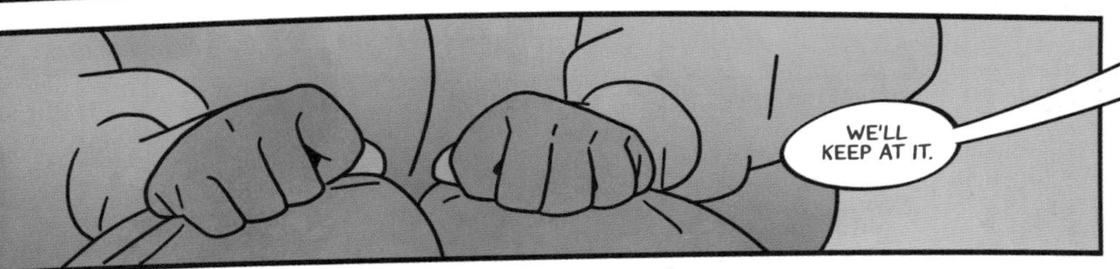
WE'LL KEEP AT IT.

OKAY...

"THIS IS A ***SKILL.*** SAME AS ANY OTHER."

"YOU GOT A LOTTA FOCUS. A LOTTA DRIVE..."

"SO WE'LL WORK AT IT."

"YOU CAN ALREADY SEE THE ENERGY THAT'S OUT THERE...."

"EVENTUALLY YOU'LL FEEL IT, TOO."

"YOU SAY THAT, BUT..."
#1 DAD

AL'S
SEAFOOD
Bar & Grill

"...ALL I FEEL ARE MY SWEATY PALMS!"

"I DON'T GET WHAT I'M SUPPOSED TO BE FEELING!"

"THERE AIN'T NO GUIDES FOR THIS, KID."
the Witch

THE BASICS OF TEACHING
So you want to be a teacher?!

"I DON'T KNOW WHAT'LL FINALLY TRIGGER IT FOR YOU..."
"FOR ME..."

IDIOT!

"THERE JUST AIN'T WORDS FOR IT..."

IT'S YOU!

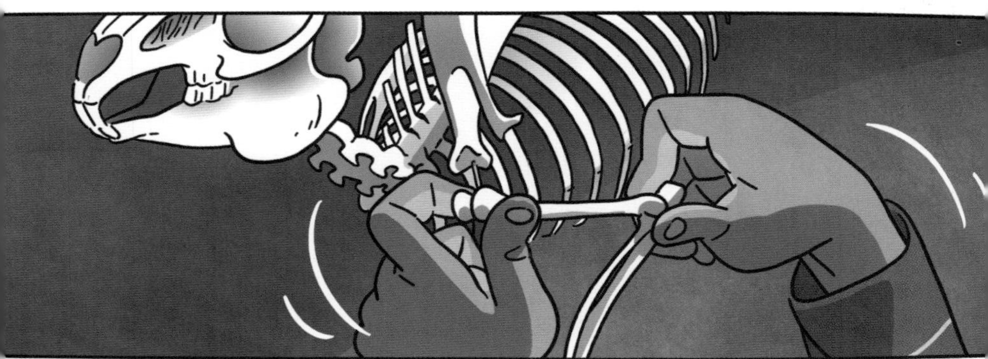

WOW!
I CAN'T BELIEVE IT'S DONE!

IT LOOKS JUST LIKE THE ONE IN THE PICTURE!

LOOKS GOOD.

IT LOOKS **AMAZING!!!**

YEAH!

I KEEP *SUCKING* AT IT, JACKS!
YOU GOTTA KEEP AT IT.
WHAT IF...

WHAT IF YOU SHOWED ME *OTHER* MAGIC I COULD DO!
Y'KNOW, NOT JUST GLOWIN' HANDS AND SEEIN' GHOSTS!
THERE'S GOTTA BE *LOADS* MORE YOU CAN DO!!

I TOLD YOU THIS HAS TO BE DONE A CERTAIN WAY.
I'M TEACHIN' YOU THE BASICS.
YOU CAN'T BE DOIN' NOTHIN' ELSE 'TIL YOU LEARN 'EM!
BUT IF YOU JUST *SHOWED* ME–

IT'D ONLY BE A *DISTRACTION!*
...

WELL MAYBE THAT'S WHAT I *NEED!!*

A DISTRACTION FROM CONSTANTLY **FAILING!!**

AND ***THEN*** ALL SHE SAID WAS TO COME OVER ON HALLOWEEN, AT DUSK.

WHAT!?

SO NO TRICK-OR-TREATING!?

IS SHE TRYING TO ***PUNISH*** YOU?!

I DON'T THINK SO.

SHE SAYS SHE WANTS TO ***SHOW*** ME SOMETHING.

MAYBE IT'S SOMETHING–

RAH!

ARK! ARK! ARK!

...COOL?

... I'LL SHARE MY CANDY WITH YOU...
I'M NOT UPSET ABOUT TRICK-OR-TREATING...

OKAY, SO SPILL!

...SO YOU HAVEN'T BEEN ABLE TO USE MAGIC YET...
YOU CAN SEE GHOSTS, THOUGH! THAT'S **COOL!**
IT'S JUST...
...THERE WOULD HAVE BEEN A **REASON!**
A REASON FOR WHAT?
FOR WHY I FEEL SO **DIFFERENT!**
WHY I DON'T **FIT IN!**
AND IT'D BE AN **AWESOME** REASON!
I'D BE A **WITCH!**
YOU NEED A REASON?
HOW 'BOUT THIS:
IT'S THE REASON WE'RE **FRIENDS!**
I HANG OUT WITH YOU 'CAUSE—**WITCH OR NOT**— YOU **STILL** THE BIGGEST WEIRDO I KNOW!
NICE EARRINGS, BY THE WAY!
YOU **FINALLY** NOTICED!
YOUR MAMA LET YOU DO THAT?

MY MOM CAN'T GET ME NEW CLOTHES ALL AT ONCE...
BUT I DO GET TO PICK OUT MY OWN FROM NOW ON!
AND MY DAD GOT ALL THESE BOOKS FROM THE LIBRARY AND HE BEEN READING AND READING...

MY BROTHERS ARE THE SAME AS ALWAYS...
HA! TOO BAD!
chew chew

NOW IF MY HAIR WOULD ONLY GROW FASTER SO I COULD DO SOMETHING CUTE WITH IT!
SEE!? I BET IF I COULD DO MAGIC I COULD HELP!

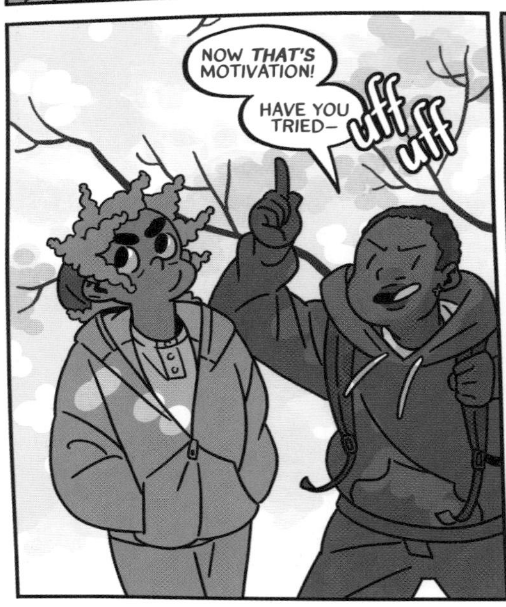
NOW THAT'S MOTIVATION!
HAVE YOU TRIED—
uff uff

—EXACTLY!
uff!
A WAND!

NOPE! NO PROPS!
JACKS SAYS THAT'S ALL FAKE JUNK ANYWAYS!
C'MON, SNAP!
LOOK AT THIS *PERFECT STICK!*
OOOOH, THIS *IS* A PERFECT STICK!

LIKE FROM AN ILLUSTRATION!
G.B. AGREES!
RUFF RUFF
DONCHA, GEEBIES?

YEAH! IF THIS WERE A *MOVIE* IT WOULD—
—*TOTALLY WORK!*
LIKE *MAGIC.*

WHAT WAS—
TELL ME YOU SAW THAT!!!
WH— NO? WHAT HAPPENED?

YOU ALL RIGHT?
SNAP?

OH MM-MM, WHAT'S THAT LOOK?
YOU TRUST ME, LU?
...YEAH?
COOL. I WANNA TRY SOMETHIN'.

FOCUS.

FEEL IT!

...
haHAH!!
WH—
WH—
HAHAHAHAHAHA
RUH
RUH
RUH
hahahahaha
hahahahahaha

hahahaha
ha ha
ha
I DON'T BELIEVE IT!
huff huff huff
DUDE! JACKS IS GONNA FREAK WHEN YOU SHOW HER YOU CAN DO MAGIC!!!
...
HUFF
KNOCK KNOCK
HALLOWEEN NIGHT
C'MON IN.

JACKS?
IN THE KITCHEN.

MAKIN' SOME HOT COCOA.
YOU GONNA TELL ME WHAT WE'RE *DOIN'* TONIGHT?
COCOA POWDER
NET WT. 8 OZ

I'M SHOWIN' YOU SOMETHIN'.
WHERE?

REMEMBER THE SPOT WE RELEASED THE POSSUMS AT?
YUP!

WE'RE GOIN' TH—
GRK!

...WHAT ARE YOU WEARING.

YOU LIKE IT?
WE WORE OUR HALLOWEEN COSTUMES AT SCHOOL TODAY!
EVERYONE THOUGHT I WAS A RAT...
...BUT I'M A POSSUM!
SEE? I'VE GOT A *POUCH* AND EVERYTHING!
–JACKS? YOU OKAY?
HCK! HCK!
JAAACKS?
HEM! MM-HM. JUST A COUGH.
LET'S GO.

I KNOW YOU'RE FRUSTRATED ABOUT YOUR LESSONS.
THEY AIN'T QUITE WHAT YOU WERE EXPECTIN'.
I DID WARN YOU THEY WOULDN'T BE.

"WHY NOT FLY OR SHAPESHIFT OR ENCHANT MY HOUSEHOLD ITEMS TO CLEAN UP?" RIGHT?
YES! WHY NOT THOSE THINGS?

I GET BY JUST FINE WITHOUT ANY OF THAT.
SO DO YOU.

WE AIN'T JUST USING THE ENERGY *AROUND* US, SNAPDRAGON.
THUD
OUR OWN LIVIN' SPIRITS.
WE'RE USING OUR *OWN.*

THAT'S WHY WE TAKE THINGS SLOW.
THAT'S WHY WE CAN'T BE *FRITTERIN'* IT AWAY ON FOOLISHNESS.

IT'D TURN US HOLLOW.

DO YOU UNDERSTAND?
YES.

GOOD. NOW, WE'RE GOING FLYING.

AH!

THERE WE GO. TAKEOFF'S ALWAYS THE HARDEST.
'SPECIALLY WITH THE BENCH.
WH-WH-WHY—
WHY THE BENCH? I LIKE TO SIT DOWN.
AND BELIEVE YOU ME, IT'S COMFIER THAN A BROOM.
NO—
WHY DIDN'T YOU TELL ME YOU COULD FLY?!?
I DON'T. OFTEN.
BUT THERE ARE CERTAIN TIMES CHARGED WITH ENERGY—
—LIKE HALLOWEEN—
—WHEN IT'S EASIER.
AND I FIGURED YOU WERE RIGHT—A DISTRACTION MAY BE WHAT YOU NEED.
RECOGNIZE WHERE WE ARE?

OH! THE SHARP TURN ON PRATTER ROAD!
"SPLATTER" ROAD. THAT'S RIGHT.
pat
pat
pat
pat
THE BUSIEST SPOT FOR OUR WORK, RIGHT?
FREEZE
WELL, NOT TONIGHT.

!!
NAH.
HA!
AGAIN?
NOD

SCREEEEEEEE
FLOP

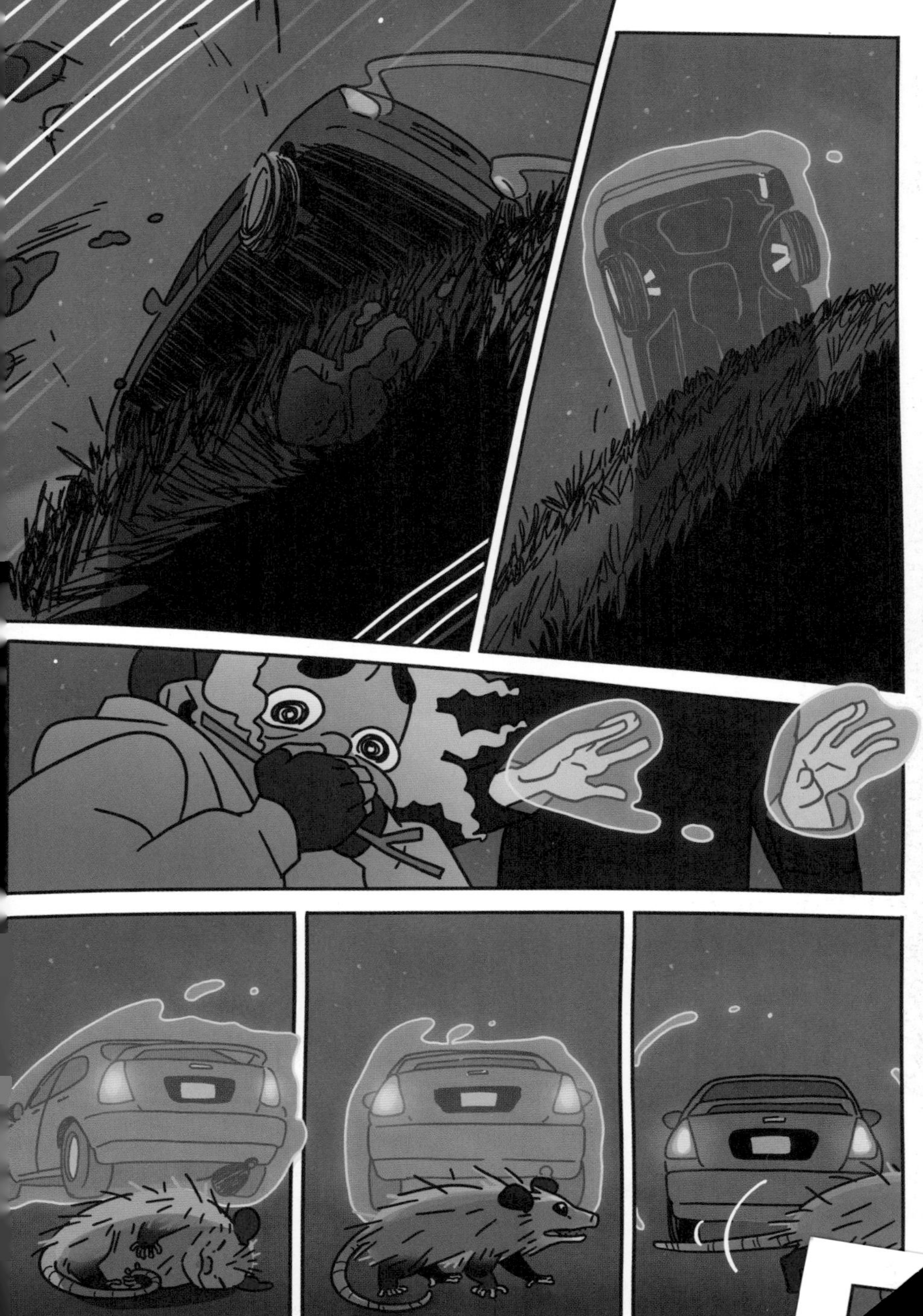

JACKS... I'M SORRY ABOUT THE CAR...THAT WAS AN ACCIDENT...
BUT, YOU SAW!
I CAN USE MAGIC!
I JUST NEEDED TO USE-
WHAT DID I SAY?

THAT JUNK DISTRACTS.

BUT IT *WORKED!*
WORKED?!
YOU SENT YOUR RAW POWER FLYING AT A CAR...

THAT WHATCHU WANTED?
NO. THEN IT DIDN'T WORK.
I BEEN TRYIN' TO TEACH YOU ***REAL CONTROL*** SO YOU DON'T ***MAKE*** MISTAKES LIKE THAT—

SIGH

I'M VERY TIRED, SNAP-DRAGON.

THAT'S ALL FOR TONIGHT.

MAMA?
YOU HOME?
Covering a late shift.
-Walked G.B.
-Don't eat all your candy at once!!
Love,
MOM
SIGH

COOL
THUMP
THUMP
THUMP

NEED COFFEE?

HERSCH! YOU'RE A PEACH!

WELL, CLASSES, WORK, TRAINING, BEING A MOM...

Y'KNOW, WE WENT HALLOWEEN SHOPPING LAST WEEK...
...AND SHE GOT GROUCHY 'CAUSE ALL THE SKELETON DECORATIONS WERE *"ANATOMICALLY INCORRECT"*!
HA! PRECOCIOUS!

SHE IS! ALWAYS HAS BEEN!

ALSO RESPONSIBLE, INDEPENDENT...
BUT... BECAUSE OF THAT...
I WORRY I'VE BEEN RELYING ON HER TO TAKE CARE OF HERSELF ***TOO MUCH***...

HEY, SHE'S A SMART KID! SHE KNOWS WHY YOU GOTTA BE GONE SO MUCH!
AND LIKE YOU SAID, ONE MORE SEMESTER!
THEN YOU'LL HAVE A SHINY NEW DEGREE, ONE LESS CRAPPY JOB, AND MORE TIME TO SPEND WITH HER.

MAYBE EVEN ENOUGH FREE TIME FOR ME TO TAKE YOU OUT FOR A ***PROPER*** MEAL–
HEY! WHAT?
I NEED A BIT MORE TIME, HERSCH.

"MY LAST BOYFRIEND WAS A COMPLETE DISASTER..."
jump
ARF!!
SNRT!!
HAHAHA!

C'MON, GEEBIES!
UFF! UFF!
LET'S GO SEE LULU'S HALLOWEEN HAUL.
WHAT D'YOU SAY?
KNOCK KNOCK
MAYBE THAT'S HER NOW!
LU?
WHAT'RE *YOU* DOIN' HERE?

HEY, KID.
...CHUCK.
YOUR MAMA HOME?
RELAX. I'M JUST HERE FOR MY STUFF.
NONE OF YOUR STUFF IS HERE!
YOU'RE NOT ALLOWED TO BE HERE!
YOU'RE NOT ALLOWED TO BE HERE, CHUCK.
RUH RUH ruh!! RUH!! RUH ruh!! RUH RUH
OH! THERE HE IS NOW!
LEAVE!

WHAT IS THIS?!
WHAT THE HELL HAPPENED TO MY DOG?!?
WHAT AM I SUPPOSED TO DO WITH THIS RUINED DOG?!
AH!
WHAM
HE'S NOT YOUR DOG! HE'S MINE!
YOUR MOMMY TELL YOU THAT?
LET GO!!

NOV
SLAM
DON'T HAVE HER NUMBER...

tch

bing!
E

IDIOT!

RARRAR
RARR
RARR
STOP IT CHUCK YOU CAN'T TAKE HIM!
RARRAR

HE STILL BELONGS TO ME, SO I CAN.
YIPE!!

LET. HIM. GO!!
ARK! ARK! ARK!!

GET OFF!
ARK! AR
ARK! AR

ARGH!
"OH, CRAP..."

NOW WHAT AM I GOING TO DO...

SNRT!!

SNRT
SNRT
...BUCK?

HEH!
RUMRUMRUM

GOOD BOY!
COME!

huff
huff huff

C'MERE!
GOOD BOY!

SNIFF
SNIFF

STAND

CRAP.

YOU GUYS SEEIN' THIS?

WHAT'S GOIN' ON, FELLAS?
YO, HERSCH!
VI!
CHECK IT OUT!

A GRANDPA IN PAJAMAS JUST PEELED IN FRONT OF THE STATION ON A MOTOR-CYCLE!

IS THERE OMETHING E CAN HELP YOU WITH, SIR?!
HAVING AN EPISODE?
SAYING ANYTHING.
HE'S JU REVVING ENGIN

I THINK I'VE...
...GOTTA GO.
VI!?
I'VE GOT A FEELING!
EXCUSE ME?
DO I KNOW—
HERE! HOP ON.
NOVEMBER CREEK FIRE STATION
NOVEMBER CREEK FIRE STATION

C'MON, CHUCK! JUST LEAVE!!
NO!! I WANNA KNOW WHAT THE HELL THAT WAS!
WHAT DID YOU DO!?!
AND-AND WHAT WAS THAT GIANT...THING I SAW HERE LAST TIME...
GIANT THING?
SHUT UP!!
YOU KNOW WHAT I'M TALKING ABOUT!!!
TELL ME WHAT'S GOING ON HERE!!
GO!
AWAY!!

OOF!
EH?

SNAP?
MAMA?!
JACKS?
SNAP!
CRASH!
CUJO!

SIC!
SNAP!!
OH HO!

GOOD DOGS!
sniff
sniff
sniff
sniff
DIDN'T TEACH HER THAT ONE...
HEE HEE!
WHOA!

ARE YOU OKAY?!
YEAH!
ARE YOU HURT?!
I'M OKAY.
ARE YOU SURE?
YES!

SNAPDRAGON.

I'M IMPRESSED WITH HOW YOU HANDLED YOURSELF, KID.
YOU DID GOOD.

...AND I BELIEVE I OWE YOU AN APOLOGY...

JUST BECAUSE YOU WEREN'T DOING THINGS *MY* WAY—
—DOESN'T MEAN YOUR WAY WAS *WRONG.*

I WAS BEING STUBBORN.

SO, I'M SOR—

THANKS, JACKS!
BUT I THINK I GET WHAT YOU WERE TRYING TO TEACH ME NOW!

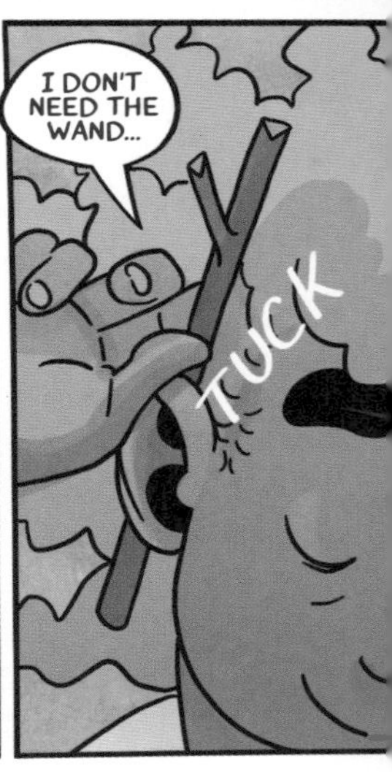
I DON'T NEED THE WAND...
TUCK

...I GOT EVERYTHING I NEED RIGHT HERE.
DON'T YOU DARE TRY TO LEAVE AFTER—

AH!!!
HA! I LIKE WHERE YER GOIN' WITH THIS. LET ME GIVE YE A HAND.
HEH HEH THANKS.
SNAPDRAGON BLOOM.

HEY!
LET ME OUTTA HERE!
HEY!
THUMP
THUMP

THREE WEEKS LATER...

"SHE'S GONNA *FREAK!*"
HEY, JACKS!
OOOH! IS THAT THE RACCOON?
MM-HM. IT'S ALL CLEANED UP.

HAHA HA!!
GOOD DOGS!
RAMPAGE
CRASH! CUJO!
GO LAY DOWN!

YOU CAN START SORTING THE TOE BONES.
'KAY!
RAMPAGE

SOOO, MY MAMA AND I WERE TALKING...

...AND WE'D LIKE TO INVITE YOU TO OUR THANKSGIVING!
UH...OH. UM...

I–
IT'LL BE AT MY GRAN'S HOUSE.

SNAP, THAT DON'T SEEM LIKE A GREAT IDEA.
WHY NOT!?
YOU COULD–
IT'D JUST BE DREDGIN' UP THE PAST.
GRANDPA DIED A LONG TIME AGO!
I THINK SHE'D BE HAPPY TO SEE YOU!
IT HAS BEEN DECADES.

DON'T YOU STILL LOVE HER?
I'LL ALWAYS–

SIGH

BUT WE BOTH MOVED ON A LONG TIME AG–
Y'KNOW, MY MAMA TOLD YOU HER NAME IS VI...
...YOU KNOW WHAT IT'S SHORT FOR?

VIOLETS.
AW, *THANK* YA, HONEY, TRULY.
VIOLET.
I AIN'T EVER LIKED A FLOWER MY ***WHOLE LIFE!***

s i g h

OKAY, NOW BRING THE FRONT PIECE 'ROUND THE ***BACK*** OF THE, *UH*, BACK PIECE.
THEN LOOP IT TO THE, *UH...*
...RIGHT!
AND AROUND THE BACK AND BRING IT UP PAST YOUR CHIN.
THEN YOU TUCK THE FRONT PART INTO THE LOOP YOU JUST MADE...
...TIGHTEN IT AND YOU SHOULD BE DONE?

IT'S ***BACKWARD AND TERRIBLE!***
I THOUGHT YOU KNEW HOW TO TIE A TIE, LULU!
IT ISN'T SOMETHING I CAN EXPLAIN OVER THE PHONE!

THAT'S ALL RIGHT, I CAN PULL OFF THIS LOOK WITHOUT A TIE.
I PROMISE TO SHOW YOU IN PERSON WHEN I GET BACK FROM MY AUNT AND UNCLE'S...
OOOR YOU COULD TIE IT WITH MAGIC!
PFT, *IT DON'T* WORK LIKE THAT.
OR, I DUNNO, MAYBE IT DOES?
JACKS ADMITTED SHE DOESN'T ***REALLY*** GET HOW IT ALL WORKS...
WELL **I'M** GONNA KEEP LOOKIN' FOR GHOSTS...
...AND TRYIN' TO GET THIS SEED TO GROW WITH MY MIND!
HA! *YOU* BROUGHT IT WITH YOU?
IF I COULD GROW PLANTS LIKE JACKS, I COULD HELP AT MY POP'S FARM!
OR WITH MY DAD'S HERB GARDEN!
OR HAVE A **NEVER-ENDIN'** SUPPLY OF ***STRAW-BERRIES!***
OR-
HAHA!
OF ***COURSE*** THAT'S WHAT YOU'D DO!

OOOH! GOTTA GO!
HAVE FUN WITH YOUR GRANNY AND YOUR GRANNY'S GIRLFRIEND!
LATER!
HERE YOU GO! RIGHT IN THE SUN!
WILL THIS BE ENOUGH CORN?
HEY, WHEN'S VI GETTIN' HERE?
THIS CHEESE IS AMAZING!
TRAFFIC'S AWFUL.
HANDS OFF THAT PIE, MISTER, THAT'S FOR LATER!
EEEEW! PHILLIP NEEDS CHANGING!
DAAAAD! ELLIE STOLE MY GAMEBOY!
IT'S MY TURN!!!
HEY, HEY! OUT OF THE KITCHEN!
SOMEONE TASTE THIS!
THERE'RE MORE IN THE PANTRY.
ARE WE OUT OF PAPER TOWELS?

MAMA, LET ME GET THAT!
OH, STOP FUSSIN'!
UH-UH! HANDS OFF!
SMK!

HELLO, MISS JESSAMINE.
MAMA? YOU ALL RIGHT?

I HOPE I'M NOT INTRUDING...

...IT WAS YOUR GRAND-DAUGHTER'S IDEA.

HOW ON *EARTH* DO YOU TWO...
LONG STORY, GRANNY!

NO ONE EVEN NOTICED I CAUGHT THE CASSEROLE DISH—

—HUSH!

WHO IS THIS WHITE WOMAN?

OUR TOWN HAS A WITCH.
JACKS WANTS TO GET THESE DUG UP BEFORE THE GROUND GETS TOO HARD.
THEN WE CAN ARTICULATE THEM DURING THE WINTER!
AS LONG AS THEY STAY HERE...
...I AIN'T GONNA BE TRIPPIN' OVER NO SKELETONS IN THE NIGHT, YOU HEAR ME?
SHE FED HER EYE TO A FOX AND SELLS THE SKELETONS OF ROADKILL ONLINE...
AAAW! WHAT IF IT WAS JUST A *LITTLE* ONE?

sniff
sniff
sniff
sniff
...SHE RESCUES ANIMALS AND PEOPLE'S PETS.
...AND SINCE THAT DAY BUCK HASN'T LEFT THE BIKE...
...I KINDA ASSUMED HE'D...***ASCEND*** OR SOME SUCH.
WHATEVER IT IS GHOSTS DO ONCE THEY FEEL...***DONE.***

SHE CARES ABOUT THE CREATURES NO ONE LIKES.
I SUPPOSE HE JUST LIKES BEIN' A MOTOR-CYCLE?
rum rum rum rum rum

OR HE JUST AIN'T ***DONE*** WITH YOU YET, HONEY.
BUMP!

SHE CAN SEE GHOSTS AND DO MAGIC (WHEN SHE FEELS LIKE IT).
HEM.
NAW, HE JUST MISSED GOIN' FAST.
WHOA!
CAN I TAKE HIM FOR A RIDE?!
I USED TO THINK ALL OF THAT WAS BULL.
NO
SNAP! WHAT ARE YOU...?!
NOW I KNOW IT'S ALL TRUE...
IT'S COOL. RIGHT?
I THINK THEY REMEMBER THEIR SHAPES...
...WELL, ALMOST ALL OF IT...

...THERE'S MORE THAN ONE WITCH IN OUR TOWN...

FIRST CHARACTER SKETCHES of...
SNAP
Hair Down
Hadn't used any reference photos yet
Perpetually grumpy Kid
OLDER SNAP (& GoodBoy) DESIGN
GOOD BOY
Sweet skull cowboy boots

Outside witch
JACKS
Inside witch
-Loose pants
-cheap sweaters
-crocs
young Jacks?
MEOWDY!
JESSAMINE
Their original meeting was going to be more tense

SNAP'S OUTFITS & HAIRSTYLES
Colors: Black, white, yellow, red
Early '00s fashion
Vi's TATTOO DETAIL
AL'S SEAFOOD
Bar & Grill
Violets Jessamine & Snapdragon flowers

GOOD BOY!
(Reference used for some)

PROCESS OF PAGE 123

STEP 1: SKETCH

THIS STEP IS PRACTICALLY PART OF THE WRITING PROCESS AS I FIGURE OUT PACING, EXPRESSIONS, ANGLES...EVERYTHING!

OFTEN PANELS NEED TO BE REFINED, BUT OTHERS I TRY TO KEEP AS CLOSE TO THE ORIGINAL SKETCH AS I CAN.

STEP 2: LINES

AFTER REFINING THE ORIGINAL ROUGH SKETCH, IT'S TIME TO TRACE.

STEP 3: FLAT COLORS

JUST LIKE IN ELEMENTARY SCHOOL, I COLOR IN THE LINES BEFORE I DECIDE ON THINGS LIKE TIME OF DAY, LIGHTING, TONES, AND HUES.

(THIS STEP IS ONE OF MY FAVORITES AND CAN BE VERY RELAXING.)

STEP 4: FINALIZE

NOW IS WHEN I MAKE ALL THE CHOICES I IGNORED IN STEP 3.

I DECIDE ON THE DIRECTION AND COLOR OF THE LIGHT AND ALL THE OTHER LITTLE DETAILS THAT COMPLETE THE ART AND TELL THE STORY.

COVER GALLERY

COVER DESIGNS WITH ORIGINAL TITLE:

FIRST CRACK AT
A COVER BEFORE
TITLE CHANGE.

(TOO SERIOUS
AND SPOOKY
LOOKING.)

First Second

Published by First Second
First Second is an imprint of Roaring Brook Press,
a division of Holtzbrinck Publishing Holdings Limited Partnership
120 Broadway, New York, NY 10271

Don't miss your next favorite book from First Second!
For the latest updates go to firstsecondnewsletter.com and sign up for our enewsletter.

Library of Congress Control Number: 2018953665
Paperback ISBN: 978-1-250-17111-5
Hardcover ISBN: 978-1-250-17112-2

Our books may be purchased in bulk for promotional, educational, or business use. Please contact your local bookseller or the Macmillan Corporate and Premium Sales Department at (800) 221-7945 ext. 5442 or by email at MacmillanSpecialMarkets@macmillan.com.

First edition, 2020
Edited by Calista Brill and Kiara Valdez
Book design by Molly Johanson
Printed in China by 1010 Printing International Limited, North Point, Hong Kong

Drawn, colored, and lettered in Photoshop with a Cintiq.

Paperback: 10 9 8 7 6 5 4
Hardcover: 10 9 8 7 6 5 4 3 2 1